'However old it might be and whatever might happen, a story is the only thing that can call out the centuries on parade and make them so brand new that antiquity becomes no farther away than just the nearest bakery, dairy or barbershop.'

When Anton closes his barbershop 'for the summer holiday', in order to clean it out, he strips the bikini from his tailor's dummy and leaves it standing out in the interminable rain. When it falls, its cracked head bleeds into the gutter . . .

The Reverend Daniel and his wife Sigrid arrive from a remote village to take up the largest parish in the city. But neither church nor the suburb it serves have yet been built. Daniel puts on his boilersuit and sets to work with the builders. Inspired by the American Forces Network, and to the dismay of the Bishop, he's soon writing pop songs alongside his hymns. But is he playing the mouth organ in the band?

Beneath the fox heads and the whale skeleton a story to last as long as the homebrewed ale is being told. A shipload of drowned sailors haunts everyone's dreams – and wreaks havoc among the 'easy and loose women' of the town. Will the elves, whose age-old rock homes are threatened by the cranes and earthmovers, allow the car park to be built?

The storm rages, intermittently and abruptly subsiding into vertically falling rain. Floods are commonplace, disruption endemic.

Einar Már Gudmundsson's story weaves seamlessly from fact to fantasy, from the seemingly mundane lives of the present day to the folk tales and sagas of the ancient past. The shifting focus creates a world of infinite possibility – amusing, touching, and alarming.

GW00371086

SHAD THAMES BOOKS

Also in this series:

Brushstrokes of Blue
The Young Poets of Iceland
Selected and with a Preface by Páll Valsson

Angels of the Universe
(Englar alheimsins)
Einar Már Gudmundsson
Translated by Bernard Scudder

The Trolls' Cathedral
(Tröllakirkja)
Ólafur Gunnarsson
Translated by David McDuff

The Uncharted Land
(Grámosinn glóir)
Thor Vilhjálmsson
Winner of the 1988 Nordic Council Literary Award
Translated by Bernard Scudder

SHAD THAMES BOOKS is the imprint for
contemporary Icelandic literature in translation
published by The Greyhound Press.

Epilogue of the Raindrops

McCartan
Jan 96

Epilogue of the Raindrops

Einar Már Gudmundsson

Translated from the Icelandic

by Bernard Scudder

SHAD THAMES BOOKS

The Greyhound Press

Published in 1994 by
Shad Thames Books
an imprint of The Greyhound Press
49 Norland Square London W11 4PZ

Epilogue of the Raindrops
Einar Már Gudmundsson
Copyright © Einar Már Gudmundsson 1994
Translation © Bernard Scudder 1994

Cover design and illustration by Börkur Arnarson
Typeset by Agnesi Text Hadleigh Suffolk
Printed and bound by Antony Rowe Ltd Chippenham Wiltshire

ISBN 1 899197 05 2

Eftirmáli regndropanna (1986) was first published in Iceland
by Almenna bókafélagid, Reykjavik.

This translation is published by agreement with
Vindrose Publishers, Copenhagen.

We are pleased to acknowledge the assistance of
the Fund for the Translation of Icelandic Literature.

This publication has been made possible by the generous
participation of the Icelandic Embassy, London.

Part I   The Ship in the Storm

Part II   Guffaws of Laughter and Palpitations

HERE COMES THE NIGHT

Part I

The Ship in the Storm

The Raindrops Arrive

Something in the Air

Blue Flashes

Thunder and lightning exploding above the dim, sleepy evening city are like countless electric guitars being played in the sky.

Everything shakes, rattles and rolls.

Rumblings like radio disturbances tumble about and a screeching like legions of untuned violins fills the ears both of those who hover, departed, and those who walk alive.

Like a cymbal struck with a table leg, a timpani hit with a log, or a rhythmless pneumatic drill trembling in the heavens.

Above the dim, sleepy evening city, everything is shaken to its foundations.

Some people feel the plates of their skulls shaking, and all around as eyelids rattle like windowpanes, the crust of the mind can be heard cracking.

Somewhere, there are pupils of eyes flickering like candelabra from wall to wall.

Somewhere, fissures run along fragile souls.

Somewhere . . .

Then suddenly.

Through the dark-clad firmament zoom fireworks the size of moons.

Zooming at such incredible speed that in an instant the moons seem to explode into the air.

Then the earth lights up with an iridescent, flashlike blue and an instantaneous glow bursts upon the houses and blocks.

Everything so bright.

Everything so radiant.

Even cats which fear the dark are dazzled by the glare and murky mouseholes light up and glow like bright halls.

The citizens feel as though they are in a gigantic compartment, having their photographs taken.

But the city.

The city itself.

Absolutely defenceless at the chilled extremity of the world, it sits like a naked tree on the ledge of a rockface, barely larger than a leaky shack or a tiny drop of water, seen through the blue-lit eye of the universe.

And the sea, the sea frothing and foaming.

Whipped and grey, it crashes against rockfaces where stunted branches tremble in shivering nakedness.

Their leaves are falling, if not already long swept afar, and in the blue-lit darkness all the houses, blocks and buildings, reinforced-concrete buildings, seem poised to be transformed.

As the brilliant light lends them the expression of haunted castles, it is no wonder if some people sense, somewhere, the creaking of rusty hinges.

The Dwarfs' Pledge and a Dream Aflame

There are white spectres stepping out of dreams, dead birds flying out of eyes.

Angels appear hovering on jet-black wings and archetypal birds of ill omen with ogres' heads visit the children who are innocently asleep in their beds in the apartment blocks.

Furious dwarfs appear to them, too, and elves with clenched fists aloft who pledge to continue building their shacks and defend their mysterious boulders at least until the foreman goes off his chump.

Then the children laugh.

Their malicious laughter fills the flats and floats out through the windows and into the darkness.

Of course their parents find this strange.

Anxiously they wonder why their children have suddenly started laughing in their sleep instead of talking.

While not far from the large blocks which in reality are many times larger than any bird of ill omen in a dream could ever be . . .

Inside a house . . .

Inside a little, white-painted house approached by a paved path over a field of clover.

Behind closed doors, walls, curtains and lit windows.

Yes, beneath the emblazoned parlour light burn both red and fiery yellow tongues of flame.

Burn, race to burn; yet not out of the walls, parlour, paintings, organ, sofa or carpets.

No.

Behind closed doors, walls, curtains and lit windows, beneath the emblazoned parlour light, a woman is asleep with a sewing needle between her fingers.

She sleeps in a dream and dreams in her sleep, dreams with erupting fires in her soul.

Dreams, unaware that she will soon wake.

The Unregistered Earthquake

And out in the evening.

Out in the dim blue-lit darkness where the windows of houses light up like TV screens on another planet . . .

While the mirrors along the dirty ivory walls of the barbershop reflect the brilliant flashes of lightning and propel them like depth charges through the fishbowls on the glass shelf.

And at the same time.

When Frimann the caretaker's cowbell lights up and glows like an enchanted clock within the glass bowl of the white school where Frimann sits by day and lost property is both handed in and claimed.

And if modern folklore is to be believed.

As soon as the stuffed gyrfalcon feels its heart beat in Herbert the headmaster's study.

Yes, that moment, both ancient dragons and guardian spirits which have fallen prey to the minting machine seem to toss deep within the earth, turn over in their thousand-year sleep and rub wrinkled dreams from their eyes with their spears, since under both the bumpy and asphalted streets of the estate, under both houses and blocks, someone is writhing in spasmodic tension with an earthquake rattling in his lungs.

Therefore the streets both tremble and shake.

And the barbershop and the school and the church and the sheds.

Everything rattles as the firmament blazes.

Some people see cars in parking lots competing at somersaults, and waking children sit on windowsills in their pyjamas looking out: don't they see the lamp-posts writhing like whales being killed?

An Implication of the Existence of Green-Clad Beings and a Vague Introduction to the Visions of Vergers

Is it not on precisely such evenings that the green-clad being, the spectre of the man with the film of ice that never disappears from his moustache, appears?

Because on such evenings.

Aren't they ideal for devious subterfuge?

Just listen to this.

Everyone who has seen the green-clad being, the spectre, is in complete agreement, so earnest in expression that none could be lying, that it not only swings the fat leg of a horse around and not only carries the lice-comb that the man with the moustache of ice is known to have had with him the night he went missing, but has also been seen carrying under his arm the head of a woman whom all the local residents knew by sight when she was alive and ran a shop with her husband.

And that's not to mention the boisterousness in the farmhouse on the other side of the library or the eyes, the poisoned gaze that has often fooled and deceived, caught motorists unawares and caused accidents or forced bus drivers to slam on their brakes.

Be that as it may, if the green-clad being is here, if it walks around bright as day and is here, won't it surely turn itself in of its own accord?

Or who else should decide?

Well, who, if not perhaps the Electricity Board, because while it does not exactly press the point, the green-clad being is not so different from other spectres and ghosts in preferring pitch dark in the sky and that lamp-posts and windows are all rolled up in the blackness together.

So that a power cut one afternoon, evening or night . . .

Little could be more appropriate.

Ahem:

While children in the apartment blocks are given important information in their sleep and other children who stay up in their pyjamas witness an earthquake which later proves so mysterious and odd that although it had been noticed by most of the residents who felt both its shaking and quaking, it neither registered in degrees on the Richter scale nor was ever admitted publicly.

But at the same time, and while a woman in a white-painted house dreams with volcanic fires in her soul, you can bet on it, countless old Adventist women with hordes of children fall into trances and at a special prayer meeting held by the vergers who hand out Bible pictures at the door of the Sunday School, scores of Bible pictures seem to plunge down through their minds and for all they can see a white finger pierces down from the blue-lit skies and, wreathed in burning yellow rays, points at them.

The Workshop Party

Of a Saddlemaker of Indeterminate Age, Bachelor Fishermen, and a Farmer with a Black Dog

Elsewhere in the same part of town.

Inside the old saddlemaker's workshop, in the midst of the dim narrow alleyways, are gathered various of the parties named in the heading above, the reason for their presence in the workshop being an intention to consume beverages there and, with them, kindle the telling of stories.

It should also be mentioned that both the architectural style and various other characteristics of the alleyways indicate that they are the oldest part of the quarter. The houses are smaller there and the trees larger, the streets narrower and shorter, and perhaps one of the most telling signs of the alleys' tenacity and age is the fact that on their perimeter the city's first and largest mental hospital was built.

But older than the houses and the streets, than the trees and the mental hospitals, is undoubtedly the saddlemaker's workshop, which some people say is like the stories that are told almost daily within its walls: at once older than all that is old and younger than all that is young.

For no one really knows when the saddlemaker came and built his workshop, and he has not aged in the slightest all the time it has stood there, and his own age is also an entirely unknown factor.

Some opine that the saddlemaker is just another middle-aged man who will stand endlessly at the threshold of his later years until one day he suddenly pops off, while others point out that if his tales are taken seriously it is a fair guess to put him at three hundred years old, four hundred or even one of the original settlers of Iceland.

Perhaps there was once a saddlemaker who leapt from letter to letter, out of a story and into the world; a story at once older than all that is old and younger than all that is young.

Be that as it may: variously on workbenches or the brown and red, hard, rounded saddles spread over the workshop floor, sit the fourteen fishermen, who by virtue of being fourteen in number and continually hanging around together are sometimes nicknamed the fourteen-man band, although their inner harmony does not extend to the sphere of music.

Instead, the fishermen work their respective boats, fishing equally with longlines and nets, catching male and female lumpfish alike, haddock and cod and saithe and halibut, even sometimes bull rout which some of them claim to be excellent fish if cooked correctly.

The fishermen land their catches at the little jetty down on the beach and sometimes push their wheelbarrows through the estate, shouting, selling fish, and they also hang the fish up to dry on racks allotted to them on the sandy waste by the mental hospital, which is most commonly known on the estate as the yellow asylum.

There they salt the fish too, drying it outdoors on the rare occasions when it is sunny. They sell the sun-dried saltfish directly through the back door of the asylum, by virtue of their private contract with the kitchen and canteen. To the east of the mental hospital, in the cluster of cottages and shacks there, the fishermen live.

No, it isn't easy to describe the fishermen's appearance, not all of them at once, because of course they differ from one another in the same way as people from all other walks of life, and accounting for each individually by name, patronymic, kith and kin and place of birth would turn this story into just another old fishermen's register, whereupon other fishermen and their relatives would complain of being ignored and even women with egalitarian ideals would rear up on their hind legs and call it blatant chauvinism not to mention any fisherwomen.

But besides owning both green anoraks and white peaked caps which they wear when pushing the fish around in their wheelbarrows, most of the fishermen are haggard with peering eyes and stretched, weatherbeaten skin, and share the characteristic that within the walls of the cluster of cottages and shacks they all live alone, unmarried from top to toe.

Such a state of affairs, the saddlemaker says, merely reflects the fact that the bodies of the fishermen house souls far too good to have wives, on which subject he feels he can speak with some authority, having had no fewer than twelve spouses in his day.

On the outside, the saddlemaker's workshop is a corrugated iron-clad shed considerably taller than a regular garage but both of similar length and comparably wide, with no distinguishing characteristics apart from its horseshoe-shaped door.

Inside, on the other hand, the workshop is boarded, clad with timber, which, if the saddlemaker is to believed, originated in one of the ancient forests that were in Iceland when the first settlers arrived.

As if that is not enough.

Suspended from the ceiling and along its length hangs the polished whale skeleton, which both shines and reflects light, and stuffed fox heads stare along the walls where also hang the skins both of exotic furry animals and the three polar bears for which the saddlemaker earned renown by felling with bear hugs the winter they walked ashore from the ice floes.

And there are also shields, ornate hilts of swords, and saddles, reins and bits . . .

Yes, all manner of artefacts that mix time together and turn the workshop into a world so completely unto itself that everything there seems to live a different life from that in the surrounding houses and the asylum by the sea.

Inside the workshop are not only fishermen, not only polar-bear skins, animal furs, fox heads and the whale skeleton, but also a living black dog following its master, a man in light trousers and check shirt by the name of Gunnar, the last active farmer known in that part of town, whose farm with horses, cows, sheep and chickens is in the valley on the other side of the park and fields.

While other farms have been either demolished to make way for houses and apartment blocks or converted into allotment sheds by the municipal authorities, his farm stands there as if this city had never been built.

The black dog lies on the floor at his toes, but unlike the fishermen who spread themselves out sitting on the workbenches or astride saddles, Gunnar is standing, leaning against a wall between two fox heads that stare like hallucinations past his ears, which, although they stand out at right-angles from his head, are said to be fine ears for poetry, since Gunnar, besides being a widower, is an acclaimed versifier, singer and dancer when the occasion demands.

Although he is an excellent teller of tales as well, Gunnar none the less always leaves the story-telling to the saddlemaker when in the workshop with him, since the saddlemaker neither leans up against the wall nor sits on a saddle or workbench, but instead on a chair, which is a throne of sorts with carved arms on a raised platform.

And the saddlemaker wears a waistcoat sewn together from countless leather patches of different colours, which, no more than the waistcoat itself, are of any consequence except that from the waistcoat hangs a gold-plated bell that the saddlemaker uses to silence his guests in the rare event of one of them trying to shout down his stories and tales.

Of Grog from the State Monopoly Store, Emetics, and Wine for the Consolation of Chickens

Old women of both sexes – aren't they always trying to ruin all good stories with their whinging mumbles, heckling and play-acting?

That's the saddlemaker's usual retort.

But here he need not have any such worries, neither of whinging mumbles, nor heckling nor play-acting.

He could even take down the bell and hang it on the snout of one of the fox heads or give it to the dog to play with.

Because here are present none but good men and true, my best friends, the fishermen and Gunnar, yes, good men and true, who, as well as being good men and true and dear souls of repute, are also Vikings for wine and trolls for drink.

At least quaffers by the grace of God, not blabbers and hecklers or trumpet-blowers with their heads full of erotic fantasies or that kind of hanky-panky.

Everyone here likes stories.

Everyone except perhaps the dog.

After all, dogs lack a narrative tradition.

But the dog's sleeping anyway like a clubbed seal.

To tell it just the way it is: dogs resemble teetotallers in so far as you can neither talk to them nor drink with them.

As can perhaps be heard there is little to suggest otherwise than that the drinking party here in session will sit the evening out, since it's no gnat's piss that's being served up and toasted with and washing down the food, dried fish, smoked mutton, flatbread and pickled meats.

My guests shall not have to put up with that old grog from the state monopoly store or colourless emetics mixed with fizzy drink, even less wines that are drunk only by slurring prims and for the consolation of crippled chickens, and that, I understand, are produced solely for the purpose of advertising tablecloths.

Well, fellows, be my guests . . . nobility of the land and fellow toilers of the waters and winds.

Cheers.

From an old herring barrel lashed between two beams which the saddlemaker has fitted with an old kitchen tap, the forbidden mead flows, homebrewed ale straight into gigantic coffee mugs, their handles scarcely smaller than those of old enamelled chamberpots.

And that's not all, because here is not only brew from the seven vats which is siphoned off at regular intervals with a hose into the herring barrel, but also freshly distilled pure alcoholic spirit, to be swigged straight out of a whole cellarful of carefully cleaned turpentine bottles, so powerful that more than just the innards catch fire.

Some magical formula must be at work here, charms like the

images of poetry which not only call forth ancient runes from the soul but also project, to all present, worlds enchanted with wonders and visions of unknown provenance.

Of Mermaids in the Gutters, or Why the Saddlemaker's Tale Ended in So Abrupt a Fashion

It is no wonder if both the sky illuminated with blue that is visible through the little skylight on the workshop roof and the rumblings that are heard intermittently like countless electrified musical instruments are, to the fishermen and farmer Gunnar, nothing but testimony to the magical influences of the alcoholic spirit and, need it be mentioned, still further evidence of how cunning a brewer the saddlemaker is.

Or is it the stories, the saddlemaker's tales, that possess this magical power, because not only do they hover over the workshop like hot cakes and turn the fishermen's ears into absurdly large elephantine lugs and farmer Gunnar's face into a single, gaping mouth . . .

But also . . .

What is it that the saddlemaker is relating, at the very moment that the blue-lit sky glows, except the air-raids he witnessed when he sailed and fought during the war.

But then.

Suddenly.

In mid-story.

With a whole bordello on his back and his arms full of screeching kids, the saddlemaker is running full pelt for an air-raid shelter in London.

Then something happens, so curiously out of the ordinary, that the saddlemaker finds himself compelled to interrupt his tale, cut the ends loose and toss away the words like cards in all directions.

Moreover, the fishermen too.

In astonishment, they get up from their saddles and jump down from the workbenches.

Against the wall, farmer Gunnar straightens up.

And his black dog.

Immediately it begins to bark.

In all likelihood this is just about the moment when the Adventist women on the estate fall in droves into trances, yes, at just the same time as the Sunday School vergers see the white finger descending from the heavens.

With a huge coffee mug in one hand and a turpentine bottle in the other, the saddlemaker stands there with the fishermen and farmer Gunnar, all bunched together, staring like a Spiritualist gathering, staring together with the dog past the whale's ribs and up through the little skylight.

There's no denying it.

It's a fact.

For an instant the blue-lit darkness seems coloured over with a yellow light and for all they can see a chariot of fire is driving across the firmament, chock-a-block with big-bosomed mermaids with flowing locks like sunbeams and lips so provocatively red that even the fishermen get a hard-on.

Drawing the chariot of fire are eighteen eight-legged horses with eyes like green jewels, immeasurably more beautiful and larger than the jewels in the mountain of glass outside the glass factory, while in the seat, with reins made from the foreskins of a long-extinct species of whale, sits a grey-bearded man occasionally bandying a very ordinary claw hammer such as is owned by handyman fathers on the estate and is sometimes taken in hand by little boys.

Each blow produces flashes of fire and the grey-bearded man seems to be cooking on tongues of the flames countless wriggling live fish, which he then swallows whole, fish hanging on hooks from a jet-black string vest the mermaids must have knitted from some of those ancient fishing-nets that have disappeared no one knows where.

The Raindrops Arrive

On the Threshold of the Cosmos

If human visions, visitations and disturbed dreams are to be believed, and the celestial spheres taken literally, we perhaps stand in the twilight on the threshold of the cosmos and time maybe exists only for the single instant when it appears to be making ready to leave . . .

When you see time dressed to the nines with a trunk in the doorway.

It waves, takes its leave and says goodbye, and the sideways glance you are given as you extend a hand of farewell becomes as eternal as the darkness.

But then that is the way it must always be, otherwise we would not be standing on the threshold of the cosmos, because the same moment that hope alights from your breast and your eyelids embrace the darkness, the traveller puts down his trunk and takes off his clothes as he turns around in the doorway.

Yet not because he has in any way given up the idea of going – time is always travelling away, hardly knowing on which side of the threshold it stands – but rather, he suddenly seems to recall having forgotten something, but the moment he begins to search can no longer remember what it was.

For this reason we stand in the twilight on the threshold of the cosmos and perhaps the riddle that someone sits down to try to solve is only the question mark that can be read from his countenance and the threshold of the cosmos, where we are standing: who can be sure it isn't just like any other old worn-down threshold on the doorstep of one of the houses or apartment blocks?

That's the way it is with the city as well.

This city, trembling now in the blue-lit darkness.

This city now being revealed unto men both in visions and visitations.

It, too, seems to be travelling away . . .

For while the ocean pounds the rocky shore where the fishermen's little boats ripple like tiny flags and beat against the quay, and where the yellow lights of the mental hospital stare, the rockface seems to crumble and the city, the naked tree, plummets with its ghostly castles from the ledge.

And who knows . . .

Perhaps a leaky shed can be seen wafted, with its tartan coffee mug on board, into the sea, the fierce, chopped sea where broken timber dances in its foaming mane, dancing as the evensong of long-extinct monks merges with the rhythm of bells into the waves.

And then.

As if the words leap out of the moment.

So fast, so sharp and in full accord with time that turns around and arrives while leaving:

Over the dim, sleepy evening city, the amplifiers seem to be turned off, the fireworks extinguished so that the dispersed fragments of the planets can integrate anew.

Like countless broken radios unplugged; the rumblings fall silent as the photographer disappears with his flashlight into the darkroom of the heavens.

Untuned violins, timpani, cymbals, pneumatic drills . . .

Everything.

All the stratospheric rowdiness.

Everything evaporates the moment the rain begins to fall.

It falls upon the tree on the ledge of the rockface, the leaky shed, the city full of ghostly castles, falls in pure transparent silver drops, which dance like drumsticks along the iron-grey tin roofs, pours down the walls of houses and apartment blocks, moistening the streets, gardens and fields.

Falls and goes on falling long after the fireworks have lost all their blue power, long after the electrified instruments have fallen silent.

Over the dim, sleepy, evening city there is no sound in the air, nothing but the dripping of the pure silver drops.

The Ship in the Storm

Inside the Little White House

The Tape-Measures of Reality

Wasn't a little white house mentioned just now, where a woman is sleeping with volcanic fires erupting in her soul?

Oh yes, but there was no mention that the little white house where the woman is sleeping with volcanic fires erupting is little only with respect to its location beside the big fifteen-storey apartment blocks, for the simple reason that both as a home and a household it is large.

And not just because it is spacious and lofty, or for the attic that can be reached after clambering up wooden steps and opening a hatch with a handle on it.

Nor that its size is calculated only on the basis of the number of people at its meal table, nor that the number of square metres has been precisely designed to yield the result that the little white house could accommodate the inhabitants of three even four apartments in blocks.

No, my good fellows.

The tape-measure that reality stretches around itself does not present its results only in centimetres and, since the little white house is the residence of the local clergyman, isn't it obvious that there is another angle to both its smallness and greatness than that determined by the apartment blocks towering above it?

Or in other words:

Where the shepherd of souls lives is everyone's home, so that all the houses and buildings feel inferior beside both the church and the clerical residence, which in the minds of the people on the estate are one and the same place and, as is common knowledge, the statistical fact of the number of square metres is powerless at the time when hearts are opened up like apartments for inspection.

Otherwise Jesus Christ would have told Peter something quite different from that stuff about the rock, and the faith that moves mountains remains indifferent to the development of architectural technology, as is best illustrated by the Reverend Daniel's parish church which is half built and only partially plastered, as well as lacking, for example, heating pipes in the walls of the children's chapel, and the double-glazing in the windows of the nave is still single, so that the old people reap nothing but pneumonia from attending church during the winter.

The same is true of the parish sanitary facilities, which resemble the Garden of Eden in so far as men and women alike urinate in the same toilet, which, while admittedly being a stylish Swedish water closet, is as common to both sexes as the grasses of the ground and the leaves and fruits of the trees were to Adam and Eve in Paradise, which is a bad thing not only because of the number of local men who urinate on the seat, but also because the arrangement has darker and more dubious aspects, such as that in the spring when serpents rise in tatty souls of children awaiting confirmation and girls with the chilling anxiety of maidenhood in their hearts encounter boys who secretively, with their virginity trembling, accidentally on purpose forget to lock the door.

The Scream in the Parlour

Be that as it may, inside the lit-up vicarage, behind the rippling curtains, on the dark-brown sofa facing the pedal organ, which stands against the wall close to the little prayer table, sits Sigrid, wife of the Reverend Daniel, in a rose-patterned dress, sleeping with her eyeballs floating dreamily behind eyelids obscured by her black hair falling across and hiding her face, while her fur-lined slippers lie willy-nilly on the floor, by her embroidery, beside her feet, which rest on the carpet.

It hardly need be stated that ever since the church was built and Sigrid and Daniel broke out of their mountain isolation and forsook the godforsaken backwater where the Reverend Daniel had served for some two decades, and moved to the city, Sigrid has stood firmly by her husband's side and been such an indispensable link in the parish work that it was no wonder that more than one and more than two children on the estate asked with their innocent blue eyes why she didn't have a black dress like Daniel too, with a white collar like his, yes, why couldn't they wear matching dresses?

Elsewhere, farther inside the parlour, at the round table, sits the Reverend Daniel. He is clearly busy, wearing reading glasses, which have slipped slightly down his nose.

And he crouches forwards.

Yet, although he is wearing reading glasses and crouching forwards, a curiously contented expression rests on his face, sometimes even sardonic and prankish.

Who knows?

Perhaps the Reverend Daniel feels suns lighting up the pupils of his eyes, within the interior of his forehead a cloud floating, which, although drawn with rather clumsy outlines, wears a friendly face, and while joyful children jump and shout in his innards a duck swims through his mind, which is calm as a pond.

On the parlour wall behind Daniel hang nothing but biblical pictures. They are identical to the Bible pictures that the vergers at the Sunday School hand out, only much larger, for it is widely believed that the Reverend Daniel paints and draws them himself and even writes the blue-lettered captions on their backs before he hands them over to the vergers for some unknown divine remuneration.

This theory is based on the fact that some of the pictures that the vergers hand out depict the Reverend Daniel in person, clearly and unequivocally, most often as one of the apostles and – without entering into an artistic critique – on closer examination of the framed biblical pictures behind the Reverend Daniel, it emerges that, besides the classical portrayals with winged angels hovering with dimples on their chubby childish faces, and apart from the pictures of Jesus Christ walking alone over bridges, Jesus can also be seen standing by the sea talking to a blind man, and the blind man Jesus is talking to is the spitting image of one of the fishermen who is at present sitting on a saddle in the saddlemaker's workshop, quaffing homebrewed ale.

Although the Reverend Daniel is transparently not in the least asleep but on the contrary wide awake, it is more difficult to tell how long Sigrid has been sleeping on the sofa.

At least it is a long while since the Reverend Daniel last heard the sound of her sewing needle, and outdoors the pure silver raindrops are beginning to fall.

With a firm but gentle beat they play against the windowpanes and perhaps permeate into the rafters of her thoughts, because suddenly Sigrid starts tossing and thrashing about, the sofa creaks and writhes, until she pricks herself on the sharp point of the sewing needle she had been using for her embroidery:

Daniel!

She screams with his name on her lips.

Daniel!

To Happen or Not to Happen

The suns seem to extinguish in the pupils of his eyes.

The cloud sailing within the interior of his forehead rains a few pearl-shaped drops of sweat which suddenly glitter.

And the pond in his mind ripples and begins to blow away.

The Reverend Daniel. It's as if he is whisked, if not into another world, then at least out of one.

He gives a start, jumps, jerks backwards so that his glasses slide back into place.

Really they are in position for the first time.

And his chair shakes and one of the pieces of paper Daniel has been attending to drops like a bird's wing on to the floor.

His heart palpitates and he feels his forehead growing hotter and reddening with the racing of his blood.

And without realizing and without understanding the Reverend

Daniel is ready to blaze up to high C and tell Sigrid off for screaming like that while he is concentrating on his work.

That sort of thing . . . i– . . . isn't it like biting a praying man in the back . . . li– . . . like . . .

But then, just as the clerical fussing and remonstrances are breaking forth upon his lips.

In a single instant the Reverend Daniel sees that Sigrid's scream was not just some feminine squeal, neither a random shout nor a crafty ploy to attract attention, because her teeth are chattering and her jaws trembling while her eyes float in some remote world where the ruins of her dream continue to burn long after they have been doused with water.

Daniel . . .

The only thing that comes to her lips is his name.

Over and again it resounds like an anaphora from an ancient gospel or an incantation that stutters and stays still for lack of both rhyme and alliteration.

Daniel . . .

Her black hair tumbles dishevelled over her ears, her cheeks flushed, her face pale and swollen. A terrified expression plays across it as she sucks the blood to stop it flowing after the prick from the sewing needle.

Daniel, what's happening?

Even though he can detect her thumping heart and the desperation in her words, the Reverend Daniel seems to feel easier on hearing this question.

Happening, Sigrid dear, is something happening?

His voice is soft, containing a clerical purr, so that if the words are interpreted and their sound made to ring through the soul, they mean that nothing is really going on at all.

And Sigrid answers:

Oh yes, there is something happening here, something you ought to see Daniel because you . . .

The words tumbling out of her are like stones that do not know whether they ought to roll up the mountainside or down it, and the

Reverend Daniel, who is standing behind the dark-brown sofa under the light that falls on his hair in shining folds, shrugs his shoulders and frowns, then looks at his watch and the pile of papers on the table, and says in a determined tone:

No, Sigrid, there's nothing going on here.

Having said those words he removes his rear profile from the sofa and moves it in the direction of the table.

But what does he know about that?

He who has almost since who knows when sat at the round table and been so busy going through, examining and scrutinizing all the homework of his pre-school pupils in the pile of papers, yes, inspecting ducklings, clouds and suns, that even though no thunder, lightning, earthquakes nor raindrops, no, none of this has exactly escaped his notice and the blue-lit flashes have even flared intermittently on the backs of his hands, his attention has none the less been elsewhere and he has paid no heed.

But, yes, in the earthquake tremors he felt a light fluttering pass through his diaphragm and for a moment felt as though the soles of his feet were being tickled.

Even less did it steal a fraction of his attention from the pre-school children's ducklings when Sigrid's needlework dropped out of her hands, in such a way that Jesus Christ's half-embroidered face fell to the floor at the same time as her head rolled on to her right shoulder, then forwards with closed eyes in the direction of her chest.

But now that she is awake with her dreams inside her head as vivid as the light of day, having screamed with her life's and soul's full might, and now that the Reverend Daniel has both come to her and gone from her, now she realizes. She turns over on the sofa, looks in the direction of the table and says:

Daniel, now I understand.

And the moment she says that, her head shakes with shivery twitches that not only run up to the roots of her hair and cock her eyes open, but also branch through her neck and down her arms like a sudden earthquake, through her whole body, making her rose-patterned dress ripple and a ladder appear at the left knee of her stocking.

What, dear . . .

As if she is bandying something away from her.

And as if she sees something she wants to disappear.

. . . What is it that you understand, dear?

Daniel asks in a soft voice from the table.

I know I understand, I must have been dreaming . . .

Of course.

Yes, of course . . .

As relieved as if they were butterflies, the Reverend Daniel caught her words in the air.

Yes, of course, you fell asleep and started dreaming.

Otherwise the embroidery with Jesus on it would not be lying on the floor and the needle, you don't prick yourself on a needle except absent-mindedly in the dark.

Yes, quite, and that's why you felt something was happening. But remember that dreams are always good, even when they are bad they are good, because they cleanse the soul of impurities, not unlike going for a swim. I think I even read somewhere they can be considered a sort of lice-comb.

So perhaps nothing happened.

Well, what happens and what does not happen, no one ever knows. If we were having this conversation in a book or on a theatre stage, it would be called something happening, but between us in our ordinary life there are only words, which the Lord sends in his mysterious ways, and as far as I'm concerned, well, I've been sitting here with the children's homework and I'm almost halfway through it and I really must say that I feel there is plenty going on there. Just look . . .

Daniel lifts up a picture of a duckling swimming on a lake with a yellow sun, white cloud and blue mountain in the background.

I wouldn't call it a Rembrandt or the sort of thing that would bring auctioneers running here with their hammers, but the remarkable thing is that all the children have drawn this same duckling from the same model and with the same sort of crayons, but no two pictures are alike. Everywhere there are individual characteristics as different as their souls. Or don't you think it's remarkable how children . . .

No, Daniel, it was still such a strange dream.

Sigrid interrupts and Daniel, who had almost forgotten she had been dreaming, is astonished at her not taking a greater interest in the children's drawings; she who for years has played the organ for them, she who has always led the craft classes and has managed to control even the rowdiest boys with her firm woman's hand, yes, even when I have lacked the nerve, she has been able to keep them sitting still cutting out pictures of kangaroos. Then she sits here with nothing in her head but a few strange events and funny dreams.

There is a hint of brashness in the Reverend Daniel's voice as he asks:

And what was so strange about it? Was I there? Were you there?

Yes, we were both there.

Oh . . .

It is probably their joint presence in the dream that suddenly kindles the Reverend Daniel's curiosity. He puts the drawing down on the top of the pile, moves it slightly, then settles back with folded arms and nods as if wishing to hear.

Perhaps he has a notion that the dream might bode an unexpected donation to the church, a lottery win or the acceptance of the application for heating to be installed. Unless it could hint at how the women's flower sale will go. Or the whist drive or the card evening. Even the minister for ecclesiastical affairs himself could be hovering there somewhere.

And into these thoughts Sigrid's words force their way the very moment she begins talking, first with a long speech and preamble in which the Reverend Daniel feels nothing happens apart from some silly darkness with Sigrid standing on an asphalted shopping arcade car park, going into the bakery to buy bread, the fish shop to buy fish and the grocer's to buy some milk.

The Reverend Daniel cannot help it, to tell the truth he thinks it is rather dull and rambling, and he darts his eyes time and again towards both the pile of papers and the clock, surreptitiously inches the chair he is sitting in towards the table and rests his arms on the leaf, clutches his right hand around his left wrist and is even beginning to think of going off and doing something completely different when his ears have suddenly started listening, since the dream is under way and has even begun to resemble a narrative in a book.

The Puddles on the Church Floor

I didn't really feel I was walking along the street until later, I just turned up, clearly heading here, on black puffs of cloud, lots of them shaped like birds, and when my feet, the soles of my shoes, touched the gutters on the roof of some house I felt my shopping bag swing into my poplin mackintosh, you know, the green one hanging in the coat rack in the hall.

And as I glide there, large as life, higher, higher, I suddenly notice I can see over the roofs of the houses, the roofs of the cars and the treetops and I sort of feel I'm taking aerial photographs with my eyes and I'm not exactly afraid because I haven't had time to be afraid but I'm afraid all the same because I know I am afraid.

This must have gone on for a few minutes until I'm suddenly standing on the street and it is damp from the rain and covered in streaky puddles as well. Then I recognize where I am because even in the darkness I know I've often walked this way before and that the field full of clover and the gravel in front of the church are there. The gravel, that's what I walk on, and the church, no, there's no mistaking it, this is the church, even though the cross and the lights on the roof aren't lit up and everything is so dark I can hardly see my hands in front of my face.

But the first thing that surprises me, I notice it the moment I walk by, is that both ropes are missing from the church bells, because, you see, I didn't feel as if I'm on my way home, I'm going to the church instead, even though I've got my shopping bag with me, since I don't recall having bought anything for the church pantry in the bakery or the fish shop or the dairy and, goodness knows, I never take my shopping bag to church without reason, just fancy the look on you vicars' faces if housewives suddenly started turning up for church with their shopping bags!

But there's nothing strange about it all the same and, compared with what I see next, that's really like any old innocent speculation or just plain mundane, because on the right of the church door, by the south wall, outside the Sunday School Chapel, no, don't you doubt for a moment that I stop dead in my tracks when I suddenly see a fire flare up and the wall, the one I've been talking about, is all ablaze.

But I don't have the slightest feeling the church is burning down and it never even occurs to me to rush in and phone the fire brigade. Of course I wouldn't have had time anyway, for standing there I feel the fire sucking me towards it or, I don't know, I walk blindly towards the flames or the flames come at me like huge paws.

And before I know it there are pink and yellow tongues of flame licking my cheeks and the closer I move the hotter and more unbearable it gets, although that's not the end of it, no, goodness knows, and cross my heart and my soul too for good measure, when I'm standing by the fire, as if it's the porch into another building, I see myself ablaze in the flames.

Yes, Lord have mercy, Jesus, Mary and St Peter, there I am all ablaze, I flare up like a rag doll, burning inside the wall, and I stand outside watching myself standing inside, and vice versa too because as I stand inside I watch myself standing outside.

Of course it's strange, I'm quite prepared to admit that, but it couldn't be clearer and when I walk closer and right into the wall to join up with myself again the fire has suddenly disappeared and I'm astonished to find myself in the Sunday School Chapel, which is all in a shambles, and there's someone there, with a blue head and wearing oilskins for all I can see, sitting down playing the organ.

I give a scream, rush out to the doorway where, judging from the noise, there might be a group of children from the confirmation class, but there's no one there all the same when I get there.

Inside the chancel I hear a service, an ordinary Sunday morning service. But there's no way it could be Sunday because I've just come from the shops.

And now I don't walk in, no, I run in, I run towards the noise and expect to see the congregation on the pews, the choir and the organist, but you're standing there alone giving the service in your full regalia, soaking wet, with your hair ruffled over your eyes.

I call out your name, shout it out, scream 'Daniel', but you don't answer and I see the church floor is covered in puddles. I stare at the puddles and see my reflection in them and when I look up you seem to be crying, the tears are pouring blindly down your cheeks.

Silence in the Parlour

Understandably, the Reverend Daniel is disappointed by the dream, by not hearing or seeing anything that might suggest a little more in the collection plate, more financial scope for the congregation, the church which in his mind is like an unfinished masterpiece.

Yes, of course he is disappointed.

Not even the minister for ecclesiastical affairs has hovered in the wings, neither a card evening nor whist drive, no flower sale, no lottery win, no, nothing to suggest the application to install heating pipes will be considered.

Or should the fire be interpreted as meaning that?

No, hardly . . .

It might just as easily be an illusion conjured up by elves and dwarfs in the rocks.

When magic rocks are blasted, nearby churches often burn.

Or . . . no, that couldn't be . . . Sigrid, no, not you, no . . .

Oh, dreams.

Aren't they just nonsense, lice-combs to cleanse the soul?

Even his reading glasses are disappointed.

The Reverend Daniel rubs his thumb up and down his wrist, blinks, squints.

As if investigating whether the tears in the dream can be called forth in his eyes.

And while he gazes into the air, thinking, the silence spreads like insecticide around the lit-up parlour.

The silence.

It hangs suspended in the glittering pearl-shaped light, in the wall lamps beside the round table, in the snow-white Osram lightbulbs, in the cheese-yellow lightshade.

The silence.

It plays on the pedal organ, soars above the little prayer table and talks to the curtains while sucking the Bible illustrations towards itself, out of their glass frames.

The silence.

It is a blind man with a stick. It plays a drum solo by the kitchen sink, flushes the toilet and turns the raindrops lashing against the windowpanes into speakers with pulpits like humps on their backs, continually raising their voices.

Louder, louder, louder, until they end up sounding like a male-voice choir singing part-song, so overpowering that even the floor-cloths cover up their ears.

Yes, the silence.

It is a dream reborn in the air.

It squeaks like a mouse by Sigrid's ear and points out to her the sewing needle and the embroidery, reminding her of the duties of the man whom she enjoys watching rub his thumb against his wrist and blink while he thinks.

Because now he is thinking about her.

Because now it is she who is important.

Until suddenly, as if he is chasing off the silent male-voice choir into the depths of the darkness, a laconic expression spreads over Daniel's face and the purring tone of his voice does not fail him when he finally breaks the silence and says, like a grandfather talking to an intelligent, understanding child:

No, Sigrid dear, I can hardly believe we have much to fear from a fire, at least not in the weather that seems to be getting up now. You can hear the rain . . .

Your words are like the wind breathing in my head, kisses bringing a blush to my cheeks.

They strike the paleness from my face, run their fingers through my hair and make my blood flow.

Say something, she says, I so like hearing you talk.

Between us are words and in the beginning was . . .

And the Reverend Daniel continues, she hears him say:

On the other hand it would be more useful to find out, since those puddles were all over the place, if the church roof has sprung a leak. It wouldn't be much fun if it started leaking in the middle of the service.

But I heard explosions too and everything was suddenly covered in a sort of darkness that's still, every now and again, pouring over my eyes.

Huh, that was just the thunder. Aren't there always explosions somewhere in the world? No, you can't open a newspaper without reading about some gas tank or oil tank somewhere blowing up. To tell the truth, I thank my lucky stars that the milk tank at the dairy has come through unscathed, then the children get their milk and I get my pictures like the ones on this pile here.

The moment the Reverend Daniel mentions the pictures he rests one hand on the pile. The hand says much remains to be done here, an attitude that is underlined by both the expression in his eyes, which suddenly turns serious, and his mouth, which he purses.

Sigrid realizes that her dream has had its allotted span for the evening.

If it made her feel better being able to talk, she feels even better still at having heard someone else talk, so that as she sits in the parlour staring into the air and listening to the raindrops, with a faint suspicion that Daniel might have been right after all in saying that nothing happened.

For isn't everything in the parlour exactly as it should be:

The pedal organ, the prayer table, the lights and the pictures.
Everything.
Yes, even the patience cards.
In the shadow of the pile of papers, they are lying on the table.

The Ship in the Storm

Of Relations Between the Local Residents and the Mental Hospital: A Few Questions on the Nature of Reality

Suddenly that same evening a terrible storm broke out, just before which some people claim to have seen an old woman, outrageously ugly, walking back and forth along the shore and turning as if to address the waves.

She was wearing a red headscarf with white spots and carried a knobbly stick with a bundle tied on the end over one shoulder, and some said her face showed wrinkles as deep and clear as the year-rings of ancient trees.

Others deny this outright, but maintain firmly instead it was an elderly man who was roaming the beach, carrying neither a stick nor a bundle over his shoulder but in its place something resembling a rake and instead of the headscarf was a hat, while some saw a tree trunk with bells on standing out of his ears.

Every time he turned his head the bells rang.

An old woman or an elderly man, what difference does it really make, for the eye-witnesses drew exactly the same conclusion from the sight, namely that here was one of the older generation of patients from the mental hospital, yes, someone either female or male had escaped from the yellow mental asylum, having patently been locked away for a long time and therefore somewhat more than somewhat strange.

Such a conclusion prompted another, an affirmation that the hospital porters had yet again demonstrated their professional incompetence, for, as a result of their neglect, the patients walk in and out of the asylum door and even have keys for their private use.

A flat denial by the hospital porters of such claims.

No, there's nothing new about that.

Nor that they resort to talking in abstractions, such as professional defamation.

That's old hat too.

And so it comes as no surprise either when doctors and nurses alike shake off such claims like any other bees in the bonnets of the local residents who, despite the fact they are free to walk the streets, are in many cases not exactly normal themselves.

Since, the fishermen's lovers, washerwomen and cleaning ladies excepted, everyone involved in the hospital operations points to the fact, which they consider themselves able to substantiate with more documents than just the senior physician's diary, that on the said day all able-bodied elderly people were assembled in the handicraft room where no less worthy guests than the entire collection of dogs from the Society for the Blind had turned up for a visit.

Burning like cigarettes, questions linger in the minds of the local residents:

Who was it walking the beach that day? Is there any old woman or elderly man here who will come forward? Or did anyone leave footprints in the sand that day?

Except, and the question has also been raised at meetings in various parts of the estate:

Could it be that the mental hospital, through some psychedelic jiggery-pokery, has expanded and thereby extended its mental jurisdiction?

Or in other words:

Can hallucinations be produced on the beach and is it conceivable in consequence that in the future there will be a handicraft room on the sea bed where starfish and bull rout alike will be cured of mental illness while dogs with waterproof lungs turn up for a visit?

Or are the senior physician, doctors, nurses and porters all nuts?

If not, as more documents than just the diary can undoubtedly prove, then what about the local residents?

And it did not eliminate certain questions or simplify the matter when it later transpired that, just like the earthquake tremors that earlier in the evening had shaken and rattled the quarter, neither the sharp gust of wind that had ferociously torn up trees by their roots nor the terrible storm that had suddenly broken that evening were ever recorded or appeared on weather maps, so that no figures can be quoted, any more than the Richter scale of the earthquake tremors, to reveal the speed in knots the storm reached.

Is it any wonder, then, if everything sometimes appears in retrospect to be no more than a trick, a lie, an illusion and a trick, as if reality were just a mirage kindled intermittently in the eyes, or a tall story transmitted on spotty tongues, a tall story in which even the unreal proves to be true while the visible evaporates.

Be that as it may, and whatever the local residents might have seen, they also know from past experience that it is safest not to go around spreading complaints about the yellow mental asylum because everybody who knows anything knows that its fingers are not white fingers of that divine ilk that the Sunday School vergers witnessed with their own eyes through the windows of the yellow YMCA building, but that instead it is like a monster with long sharp claws, pincer-like claws that track people down through the darkened alleyways of the mind, even in broad daylight.

Of the Storm Raging Along the Streets and of Heroic Men in Anoraks

But now it is evening and the storm raging along the streets carries with it a question that can be answered only by looking out to sea, the fierce, chopped ocean whose foaming mane of wild denizens of the deep lashes the rocks where terrified gulls lose their senses as the sea floods on to the beach to drench the sand that glitters for an instant in the outwash.

But, looking out to sea, it bursts aflame like a match in your eyes, this question, the same one burning here on the lips of the words, the same one you can ask only if you hurry to where the best view can be had:

Yes, what is that ship rolling offshore in the waves beyond the asylum, not so far from the little green isle where the monastery still stands, even though the monks have long since vanished and live only as departed spirits in a wind that occasionally dons their dirt-brown cowls?

But when the monks appear, there is the pealing of bells resounding in the waves, jingled in prophecies by belts threaded together from the bones of birds. At such times the doors to the monastery stand open and it is said that lost seafarers are guided from hazard to harbour.

But this evening the storm has not only slammed the monastery doors shut and locked all the monks inside, but is also breaking waves over the ship while the greatest surf in living memory swirls around like a blizzard.

Even though some people might surmise this is only yet another mirage, the ship simply a mistaken vision like the old man and woman or even a delusion developed by the senior physician like a photograph in the ocean.

No, there's definitely no mistaking it, for so many of the local residents see how the ship plunges in the sheer cliffs of the waves and how it rocks and is tossed and turned like an uncontrolled citadel around itself.

Rocks back and forth and up and down until the mast standing straight up into the air snaps, flops down and becomes nothing.

The first people to see the ship are naturally grown men and women who are still awake in the large apartment blocks and flock in droves to their windows, some with telescopes that clearly and faithfully reproduce the image in their eyes.

The most heroic of the men put on woollen socks, fur-lined boots and anoraks, then knock at the doors of houses that do not have a view to the sea, where other men, also heroic, are also dressing to encounter the weather.

And now it is evening and the storm raging along the streets approaches from all directions at once and the crystal-clear raindrops, instead of falling down straight as if custom-built for umbrellas, are swept horizontally and explode against each other.

In some places there isn't a cat in hell's chance of moving a step forward; not backwards nor forwards nor to the side. In their heroism the men in anoraks are sometimes forced to stop.

Or more precisely:

They are stopped, for here there is no way to turn away from the storm and turning back is a hopeless course, all that can be done is to forge ahead without moving a step forward, so that no matter how the heroic men stand the raindrops lash them and their faces are ruddy from the water, cold and grimacing.

A Card Evening at Full Pelt

But without the Reverend Daniel being surprised by her.

Without her disturbing him to any degree.

No.

But Sigrid.

She cannot remember what she has been thinking when she feels the gust of wind that does not only move like a living being through the house slamming the doors behind it . . .

No, also . . .

Somewhere in the vicinity she thinks she hears cars crashing into each other and through her mind, past the window, a tree is swept, shaped like a disfigured bird.

So that's the storm, she thinks.

That's what it's like, the storm.

Visualizing it, she senses this is the same storm that turned up on the cards at the last card evening they held with the parish women, when they all shook their heads in disbelief because the cards showed so many men running at full pelt without any suggestion of them being at a sports meeting or in a relay race which could in a certain sense have been interpreted symbolically. The storm, that's what the storm's like.

Now she sees it, feels it and hears it.

But the dream I dreamed just now, what can the dream mean then, she thinks in the silence as the raindrops step up their beat and suddenly begin pounding on the windowpanes like savages on drums.

Or is it ball-bearings used as cannonballs in a game of tin soldiers?

Or hailstones the size of knucklebones?

Or . . .

Sigrid sees nothing through the window, nothing but the lit room reflected prosaically back in the glass, seemingly full of teardrops swimming with the Reverend Daniel about the round table.

She also notices the vague lights in the windows of the apartment block but when she strains to look at the drops the lights stretch out like tiny suns.

Stunted trees are swept to and fro in the garden, and their rushing – in the storm it conveys a sound not unlike that made by little boys who fidget and scratch at the spring under a tin drum, while the branches . . . yes, are they not swept to and fro, swept away like the shivering sleeves of oilskins being sewn in a clothing factory on the other side of time?

But who's that making something?

Sigrid pricks up her ears and in the ticking of the seconds she seems to hear countless blows of a hammer from the rocks and a distant choral song is wafted through the air, so far away that her mind instinctively changes tack.

Of a Resourceful Farm Labourer and a Crotchety Prison Warden

Just like earlier that evening.

When the blue-lit sky revealed its countenance in the little attic window of the old saddlemaker's workshop; at precisely the moment when the drinking bout rose to its feet and a formal toast was made to both newly distilled spirit and homebrewed ale . . .

Once again, when the storm arrives and the corrugated-iron-clad walls of the workshop suddenly begin to tremble, the saddlemaker leaps to his feet.

He is so sprightly and nimble that when he accidentally catches his heel on his ancient story-teller's chair, he whisks it so high into the air that in order to prevent it being pulverized by the fall he is obliged to catch it with his left hand, because in his right he is holding a turpentine bottle full of pure spirit with a huge coffee mug dangling by its handle on his thumb.

His left hand, by contrast, is free, because the saddlemaker uses it to gesture when telling his stories; he has a theory that story-tellers are almost without exception left-handed.

But enough of that.

Inside the workshop everything is shaking and trembling. The stuffed fox heads fall from the walls in droves and roll across the floor, as the whale skeleton writhes and rattles so that not just the fishermen but farmer Gunnar as well, they all think a whole whale is in the process of reincarnation, while the walls emit a not dissimilar sound to rusty nails, older than the oldest nails known to man, being extracted by magnetic force.

Amid all this commotion the men rise from their seats and farmer Gunnar is taken so much by surprise that the swig of hooch on its way into his mouth spills on to the dog, which goes wild and pounces, barking, on to one of the fox heads.

But instead of interrupting his story, as he had done when the fiery chariot of mermaids appeared at the attic window, he goes ahead regardless, talking as he catches the chair with the trembling walls trying to drown his words.

But what story is he telling?

Isn't it the tale of the farm labourer who thought he had a cure for all ailments?

The farm labourer who bet the farmer that by looking into the eyes of his cows he could cure them of rinderpest, murrain and post-natal depression.

And didn't they recover, costing the farmer a bottle of spirits, which the labourer drank while explaining how to eradicate the backache suffered by the other workers on the farm.

The farmer's ears grew and the labourer continued that a surefire way was to smear lard along the vertebrae, as surefire a way as reading the sagas to dogs on heat to stop them behaving like idiots.

And so on endlessly until the story of the resourceful farm labourer is done and followed by the story of the crotchety prison warden who was killed by the ghost of a horse.

And the newly distilled spirit flows, the oleaginous ale pours, pours into the huge coffee mugs and in such heavy streams that it is hardly worth the bother, quite pointless in fact, to turn off the tap on the herring barrel, which time and again is filled with ale from one of the fourteen brewing vats.

And since, outdoors, the storm is blowing and the workshop is creaking and shaking, it is not surprising to find the saddlemaker suddenly on the moors where stories light up about ordeals against the elements, at the same time as his eyes, his huge wide eyes, begin to sink like dim clouds, not through drowsiness but rather because the narrative slows down in this way to become dimmer and heavier.

The Ship in the Storm

Then, at last.

Weatherbeaten, the heroic men have finally reached the shore and can now see that there is no mistaking it, neither their eyes nor telescopes have wrought reality out of shape.

Their faces red from the cold, out through the hoods of their anoraks, they watch the ship rolling in the waves and the breakers crashing over it and the sailors who wave with their hands or shout with their mouths so wide open that the darkness encompassing them is one black gullet.

Or they do both at once, wave and shout. Above them, helicopters hover with dangling rope ladders, and rescue squads in luminous jackets are trying to shoot lifelines out to them.

But the sea is so rough and the foaming waves so fearsome that even though the heroic men offer their assistance, no rescue can be performed.

The rope ladders are blown back out of grasps and what happens to the lifelines no one can tell.

And the bystanders on the beach can do nothing but watch what is going on; the crazed, desperate shouts for help that drown in the thunderous seas and the sailors who gradually disappear overboard.

But when all the sailors, the entire crew, are patently, at least in accordance with all laws governing the respiratory system, both dead and drowned, something wondrous happens.

The rescue workers and heroic local residents are stunned into silence.

Yes, as suddenly as it broke, the storm falls still, and as if nothing had happened the crystal-clear raindrops begin to fall vertically again, so wondrously straight as to occasion the use of an umbrella.

Not only does the storm fall still, for at the same moment the ship seems to come back to keel, to overcome its rolling, and turn around, heading not out into the ocean but straight for land, sailing towards them under its own power.

Astonished and wide-mouthed, they all stare, for, as if guided by an invisible hand, the ship sails up on to the beach and comes to rest there like an overgrown beached whale halfway between the slipway and the mental hospital.

No matter how the beach was combed, no bodies were found; none of them was found – ever.

Yet . . .

When some of the heroic residents intend to go aboard and inspect the ship with their own eyes, they hear heavy thuds from its belly, heavy thuds with clanking and deep booming voices.

You bet.

For a mere instant there is a glimpse of the bottoms of the heroic men's shoes as they run like a whirlwind, wearing anoraks, each back to his respective home.

Part II

Guffaws of Laughter and Palpitations

Here Comes the Night

Here Comes the Night

Signpost Wanted

Isn't it surely late into the night?

Time to close the gates of the parks.

The doors of the houses.

The eyes of the heads.

Yes, surely it is.

If it wasn't, the park-keeper wouldn't be going to the park in his uniform with a torch and keys.

Or the lights of the houses and apartment blocks, they wouldn't be fleeing in such haste into the darkness.

Into the night, sleep and darkness.

And the calendars on the walls . . .

Now they are up and about and beginning to turn their pages.

Racing each other to snap up the viewing rights to the next day.

That's why.

In the darkness of the countryside and the chopped seas alike.

In the dim city and here on the estate.

Everywhere it is late into the night.

Between the leaves in the park, in a tale of misadventure told in a workshop, within a woman who does not know what to think when her thoughts stop coming to her.

Everywhere.

Also around the ice-cream machine in Siggi's shop, among the abandoned coffee flasks in creosoted worksheds, in garage repair wells and refrigerators.

Even among loose women.

In heads, in houses, in parks.

Everywhere.

If anyone owns a sign saying HERE COMES THE NIGHT it would not be a bad idea to hang it up.

Jangling and Shaking Keys

Before, when the uniformed park-keeper turned the handle and opened the doors to the house between the trees, he saw that the storm he had so clearly heard rustling the trees while he found his torch and keys had completely disappeared from the park.

And the air, the raindrops and the darkness in the air, everything was as before, as if nothing had happened.

Strange, very strange, the park-keeper had thought, standing on the platform at the top of the steps and looking out at the trees, adjusting his peaked cap instead of scratching his head. The cap has a golden braid above its peak, beneath the council workers' emblem.

The park-keeper is wearing clogs that turn as he locks the door, whereupon he walks down the steps with his torch and his jangling keys, dressed in an old long raincoat which now and again rubs between his knees.

After a few moments he has disappeared between the trees into the wood and is walking, jangling his keys, along one of the red paths that lead up to the park gates like a maze, meet at lonely places, in nooks and crannies, in a world that, full of hiding places, conceals itself among the trees.

But when night comes and the clocks announce the closing time of the gates, the uniformed park-keeper always walks these paths alone, with his torch in his raincoat and his bunch of jangling keys on his thumb, and inside the house among the trees there is not even a wife waiting for him with closed eyes asleep in the double bed.

Some people maintain one of the young gardeners kidnapped her and they were seen in a car driving out through the main gate.

Well, who knows?

Perhaps the park-keeper is only looking for her when he shines his torch to light up among the trees at lonely places, in nooks and crannies, and who can tell if he doesn't just think they only went out to buy some rakes and aren't back yet because it's always so busy at the garden tools shop.

No, it's not such a simple matter, for when the park-keeper shines his torch he also knows it is here in the park that the shadowy sides of the estate often hide away, so it is safest to take a look everywhere.

Inside the iron-grey wastepaper bins, behind the statues, under the benches, and in the flowerbeds where it is said that even the worms know him by sight, and he also looks among the flowers and trees; activities might be concealed anywhere that are better suited to darkness than daylight.

No, it is not only teenagers in inopportune love-making or kids smoking furtively, but also anorak-clad worm-thieves and housewives pretending to be sleepwalking when the park-keeper catches them red-handed with whole beds of flowers in their arms.

He has also met burglars engaged in disquisitions over their swag, seen the naked postman wearing nothing but a necktie, taken the mad telephone engineer by surprise and even seen consenting adult males standing pressed against each other with their pants around their ankles.

Dewed leaves stroke across his mind and while the gates close one after the other and lock, clear silver raindrops fall over the shoulders of his raincoat and while they click against the peak of his cap and dance at his toes there is nothing to be seen in the darkness and no suspicions that awaken until suddenly, by the lawn that, surrounded by dwarf birch and pine shrubs, is shaped like the club card-suit.

The branches crack, their whishing can be heard.

Instantly his torch leaps out of his coat pocket, its eye lights up and a beam of light plays across the soil as somebody runs between the trees.

No, shush.

Not somebody, but some bodies.

At least, countless legs amass in the beam of light and for all the park-keeper's shouts that the gates are being locked now and the park is closing, there is nothing to suggest that his words strike ears that can hear.

No, there is nobody who answers.

Just footsteps crashing, resounding and whishing.

Perhaps the park-keeper thinks he has nabbed some burglars and all that remains to be done is to corner them and collar one to give the police something to work on.

At least, he turns off the torch, hurries along the narrow path wet from the rain, over the lawn with its leafy crannies and straight ahead, through gaps between trees and on to new patches of grass, then right down a path and into the arched, gravel-surfaced tunnel.

And then press the button and turn on the light and surprise them all because now he has overtaken them and is approaching them from the opposite direction, where he can see between the trees, can see the darkness that lights up the moment he turns on the torch.

Then turn it straight back off again, because instead of catching criminals under cover of darkness and night, for all he can see there is a large group of curiously stiff men in oilskins between the pine shrubs, so green that they could be rowan trees planted by the roots inside wellington boots.

The same way he had come, the park-keeper runs back, hurries to close the final gate with his heart like a drum that cannot stop pounding, and the heels echoing between the trees, past the statues which at precisely that moment are accustomed to wake up and step out of their forms.

Or until he eventually finds a bench to throw himself upon, catches his breath and thinks, no, it can't be, either they were some jokers returning from a fancy-dress party or it was a delusion, the raindrops made the trees look as if they were wearing oilskins.

For everything can assume a human form, especially when it is late at night and you are so tired yourself.

So the park-keeper has almost regained his composure when he gets up and has even started to feel the afforested solitude in the trees, hear the rustling in the grass and echoing voices of the paths, until he approaches the arch-shaped tunnel once again; the lawn shaped like the club card-suit.

Then his heart seems to tug and he unconsciously quickens his pace, following only the widest paths. No, not the crooked detours, the black-clad cinderpaths or the secret tracks that in moments of solitude he himself has mentally trodden between the tree trunks.

He walks on, quickens his pace, walking without lingering by a single flowerbed, not a single wastepaper bin, not a single bench, without looking or prying, walking straight ahead to the greenhouse where he opens the door with its white-painted frame.

He steps into the warmth that radiates from the pipes and checks the ornamental plants with their Latin names and hurries to water everything that needs watering before he disappears outside again and closes the door behind him, then proceeds along the wide paths and vanishes into the cluster of trees where his house stands.

It is difficult say whether the keys are jangling or his hands trembling. Only that when he finally manages to open the door he feels the darkness accompany him in.

The Chronology of the Wilderness

And the night.

The night walking with the park-keeper through the door to his house.

It is not only lying over the park and the houses and apartment blocks on the estate.

No, it must surely be everywhere.

On unscalable mountainsides, in the swirling blizzard, in trickling brooks that can never be found and springs that, when all is said and done, turn out to be mirages.

The night.

Today it's in the same place it was yesterday.

On the sandy banks of the wilderness where an uncrossable expanse reigns and solitude stretches, devoid of even a single blade of grass, in all directions.

Sometimes it is also night-time during the day and people wrestle eternally with the darkness within their heads.

It seeps, pitch black, into the workshop, sometimes white from the swirling blizzard and with snowdrifts in its eyes, but mostly black all the same in the ordeal the saddlemaker has been recounting.

And still is recounting, both because it is a long tale and because inside the workshop the alcoholic silence stretches out the words into a yarn that, as it warms, also enhances the understanding of everyone who listens to the cold.

The fishermen feel the shivers without being cold in any way, no more than farmer Gunnar who in the swollen red twilight of distilled spirit sometimes sees in flickering images how the workshop has metamorphosed into a hut, a hut that a lost traveller is trying to find up on the moors.

Or they hear the man knocking, see him standing outside, and sometimes they linger over the tracks from which the search parties are beginning to stray in this eternal night.

How was it?

Hadn't the man simply gone to fetch a few stray sheep from the mountainside above the farm or had had an errand to attend to in the neighbouring district?

Be that as it may, he had waved goodbye, well prepared for his journey, wearing three sets of woollen underwear, four pairs of socks, thick wadmal trousers and more than one woollen pullover.

For all this he can thank his wife, who is clairvoyant, but naturally incapable of telling her husband to wait with his plans until the following day.

Otherwise the tale wouldn't be worth telling, so that the feminine instinct of foresightedness perhaps serves no other purpose than to underline the folly and daredevilry of men.

Accordingly, the man who had originally intended to return at dinnertime the day he set off has roamed blindly over hill and dale, far and wide, for so many weeks that if he has not crossed the length of the country he must have travelled its breadth.

And his fingers are blue and swollen, his toes like fishermen's gloves, and the loss of direction and yearning to sleep so intense that the heels of his long-since-ripped boots have no other feeling than that they are walking over the ice-cold waves of the ocean, and he has walked seven times around the mountain that is visible when not obscured by the blizzard, in the good faith that he is always forging ahead and is on his way back to habitation.

And listen now, for the saddlemaker describes the lost man's behaviour in such detail that he sometimes seems to have been there with him, or is even the stray traveller himself, and his appearance, his countenance, bearing and features, even his epigrammatic childhood retorts, all are so transparent that it is hardly surprising when one of the fishermen grabs the chance to ask a question during a short pause in the narrative when, to wet his whistle, the story-teller stands poised to quaff a whole mug of homebrewed ale.

Hey, tell us, when did all this happen?

The saddlemaker does not just choke on his ale, spurting it out in arcs through his nose, mouth and ears; he also indicates in no uncertain terms his disapproval of the question, for with a not dissimilar vehemence in his voice to when he refers to old women of both sexes who have destroyed the national art of story-telling, he asks back:

Since when have the wilderness and getting lost hung dates on themselves?

No no, I didn't mean, said the fisherman, you just seem to remember it so well, er, as if it happened yesterday.

Oh no, it's at least three hundred years since that man's bones turned to dust or four hundred or five hundred or who can tell.

Well . . .

But who can say all the same that it didn't happen yesterday?

What . . .

I ask you, is there any difference if the same thing happens at one time or another?

What . . .

Perhaps you want to make a journalist of me and you reckon tales of ordeals are just like any accident reported in the newspapers and that I'm here with my barrelful of ale and bottles of spirit like some official from the lifesaving association.

What . . .

No, I'd rather have the little boys that live around here with that earnest glint in their eyes asking which of the saga heroes I liked the most when I knew them all.

Yeah.

You should model yourselves on them.

How . . .

The trouble with those kids is that you can't even give them a drink without getting that riff-raff chasing you, their parents and that damn fool vicar and that bloated ogre that runs the school.

The Slippers by the Bedside

The park-keeper is thinking that he has been asleep for ages behind the door to his house among the trees when he suddenly starts to hear, as clearly and distinctly as when he heard the storm rustling in the trees, that the potatoes stored in the basement below his flat seem to be moving around.

They roll across each other as if jumping along a conveyor belt and into a grading machine, or tumble around playing chase, and the park-keeper, under the impression that he is asleep, also hears the big washing-machine start pacing the floor, stamping about like a nimble gymnastics teacher and a lame old woman by turns.

And, at regular intervals, heels thump with bootlike sounds against the inside of the furthermost wall, so that really it can mean only that someone is swinging on the washing-line.

All the while the hoes tremble and the watering-cans roll with grating metallic sounds that echo all over the house just before the park-keeper hears footsteps approaching up the stairs from the basement.

A door opens in the hallway and just before the bedroom door is dashed open a great commotion emanates from the kitchen with countless slurred voices as if they are speaking their words while chewing the yolks of eggs.

With a lump in his throat, the park-keeper feels nauseous in bed and is on the verge of vomiting as he tosses about with his spotted quilt on a never-ending journey across his body.

He thrashes back and forth about the bed, starts up, gasps for breath and is ready to give up the ghost, for suddenly the bedroom fills up with voices and by his bedside stand the men whose faces he saw between the pines in the park.

Looking ugly and imposing, they threaten and abuse the park-keeper, and he thinks now they are coming to thrash him with wet fishermen's gloves, piss over him and strangle him, when his eyes snap open and he wakes up panting for breath and bathed in sweat, his heart rushing like a prize stallion that has kicked over all the hurdles and gone loco.

He can still hear the slurred voices with yolks of eggs in their gullets and senses a salty smell in the air, but can see no one, no faces, no oilskins, nobody, nothing.

And the watering-cans, the hoes, the washing machine and potatoes.

Everything in the house is silent.

There's no denying that the park-keeper feels such relief that he is no longer in the slightest sleepy.

He tries to close his eyes but cannot sleep for relief, for the smiling calm that now plays about his soul.

So he dashes away the quilt, takes off his sweat-drenched pyjamas and leaps out of bed to find another pair, intending to put on his slippers by the bedside and walk around a little.

But then . . .

No.

He can hardly believe his eyes.

For instead of feeling his soft slippers swallow his toes, his soles and his arches, he treads in a puddle and sees, the moment he feels the chilling water course like a current up his body, that the carpet on the bedroom floor is soaking wet.

The same goes for the mat outside the door, the kitchen floor, the stairs and the basement:

It's exactly as if someone had been roaming around, drenched to the skin and wearing leaky wellington boots.

Ancient Cairns and New Times

A drift of snow is sweeping above the fishermen's heads and farmer Gunnar feels for an instant he is catching a cold, but the strange thing is that, the moment the saddlemaker chokes on his ale and sees himself compelled to begin his explanation of the curious timelessness which dwells in the narrative, he seems to lose all contact with the tale that has been flowing from his lips and instead of continuing with it and describing whether the man was dying in the snow or whether someone came to rescue him, he says of the story-teller's art:

However old it might be and whatever might happen, a story is the only thing that can call out the centuries on parade and make them so brand new that antiquity becomes no farther away than just the nearest bakery, dairy or barbershop.

Because all slaves to fashion, whatever name they go by, journalists, radio announcers, psychiatrists and teachers, are like ancient cairns or extinct species beside the heroes of old and the stories that have always been told, no matter how they wave around their identity cards, insurance cards, wallets and battered old cars just like the sagas have never happened and reality is just fiction and put that in your pipe and smoke it and cheers.

No, the saddlemaker is not exactly jeered and no protests break out in the workshop, but it is more difficult for the fishermen and farmer Gunnar to accept that a tale that has been begun is not finished.

In their eyes, that is like leaving dregs in a bottle or scraps of food, and they feel face to face with life with a lost man in their souls, someone neither dead nor alive, lying with his swollen fingers in the snow and his toes buried in a drift.

What happens? Does he merge with those ponderous tracks, far from the graveyards of men, or does help arrive in time? Is it not an irrevocable demand, even the collective right of fishermen waving their coffee mugs, and of the one man in the quarter whose relationship with cows and grass is more than just through the dairy co-operative, to know what happened?

No one denies that, least of all the saddlemaker who has sat down again holding his coffee mug in the story-teller's chair with its pillared arms after three swigs of hooch so huge that tongues of flame stand out of his ears mightier than if a Bengal match had been struck and the whole assembled company farted in unison. And a kindly expression came over him which, although reconciliatory, is prankish enough that the tale cannot avoid changing gear and altering its form and style.

At least . . .

Instead of disjointed divine words flowing from his lips and death being revealed to him in the conventional manner, the man stands up, with swollen fingers, puffy red frozen elephant's ears and icicles on his cheeks, and like any other wonder of nature immediately begins to do keep-fit exercises, warming himself with the thought that he will be playing an accordion when the ogres who want to wrestle with him turn up, together with their ogresses.

The man wrestles with the ogres and fells four of them, then copulates with two ogresses before being invited to a banquet where fourteen one-eyed frost-giants sit at a long table and mermaids with flowing locks play the flute and captive farmers' daughters under spells serve at table. The choir is conducted by a farmer in a check shirt and when the ale is served in barrels everyone says cheers and starts singing.

A tumultuous celebration erupts and the music resounding out of the volcanic crater of the mountain where the banquet is held seems to be continued centuries later, at the moment when the workshop begins to echo and the darkness above the depths fills with song.

Housewives wake up in droves and angrily wield telephones, although they know just as well as the duty sergeants on the other end of the line that the merrymaking in the saddlemaker's workshop will not be stopped until it has come to an end.

Snatches of Memories in the Twilight
of the Mind

Of the Storm's Influence upon Sigrid

When Sigrid comes back to earth she has a feeling, she cannot tell what, of a piercing pain, a common or garden ache, or rheumatism.

The gold-entwined light pierces her eyes.

The dark-brown sofa hard as rock.

She can feel the springs beneath her buttocks and an uncomfortable lump in her back.

Then she yawns and sighs, shakes her head at these weird thoughts and stares at the windowpanes, exactly as surprised as everyone else, the park-keeper and the eye-witnesses on the beach, in short everyone who has seen how suddenly the storm lulled.

For although it has not touched her in any meteorological sense, neither swept her away like the daredevil men in hooded anoraks nor ruffled and blown her hair, its whining violence none the less seems to visit upon her.

As if the storm has rushed through her veins, tugged at the roots of her hair and blown turbulent life into her breast.

Thus Sigrid feels her heartbeat, how it quickens between her breasts, making her rose-patterned dress ripple, and as soon as the beating of hammers has faded from the hills and the distant choral song has passed by, no sooner said than done, before they tear themselves free and take to flight, she feels her thoughts thrashing about and wallowing as if in a swelling sea.

At first they are so confused that there is no way to comprehend them. But after fluttering about distractedly, as if the storm with its hallucinations bumps slap bang into the vicar's wife, her thoughts take a clearer and more distinct course, assume the form of a story and instead of flying about soar along straight paths.

In other words:

Her mind suddenly begins to seek out familiar haunts and places so overgrown with memory that from time to time Sigrid has trouble finding her way, and since everything is so vivid and bright she sometimes feels that this garden, this mental plot of her memories, has already been visited by someone else who has dug up all the weeds.

Or is the past simply so bright because it is past and can thereby without a hint of bitterness bathe itself in the distance of that which was, and even turn disappointments into smiling reflections?

At least, while the storm is beating against the outside of the windowpanes, Sigrid feels how time – virtually every single moment she can recall, and not recall as well – starts running backwards through her open eyes until it swerves and begins flowing in the opposite direction, forwards.

And what need for eye-witnesses then; is it not clear for all to see that the days when she first met Daniel, are they not rising larger than life out of their depths?

Suitcases Full of Miracles

When this happened, Sigrid was barely a marriageable young girl in her father's house, to quote the literary style of that time, or a young grammar-school girl whose life's ambition was no more complex than, wearing the obligatory peaked cap, to matriculate out into the summer a year after that spring.

But it just so happened that around the same time a young man graduated from the theology department of the university by the name of Daniel who along with seven of his cohorts was ordained into the clergy the same day, and was so proud of his title that it is said he had a cassock tailormade and wore it not only in coffee shops but also at crowded public places where the city authorities had set up benches.

Bearing in mind these two facts, that is to say the young grammar-school girl and the newly ordained clergyman; can it not be inferred by means of the technique that has been named 'two plus two make four' that it was at one of the spring gatherings of the young Christians' associations that their inclinations first turned towards each other?

Wouldn't it be suitably typical, and realistic too, for Daniel to have turned up at the Christian summer camp as a group leader and in the guise of a clerical Galahad lured the nubile wench into a secluded meadow?

Indeed.

But none the less that was not how it happened.

There are no summer camps in Sigrid's and Daniel's love story.

Not even a sleeping-bag, rucksack or tent.

Instead, chain dances, psalms and application forms for vacant benefices.

In other words:

It began at a dance given by the new ordinands and advertised beforehand with a rumpus that outraged the majority of older clergymen, in particular the rumour that the young vicars with Daniel leading the fray had marched clad in their cassocks through the city, not only handing out announcements about the dance but also blaring out pop songs to draw attention to themselves.

But notwithstanding all of the scandal.

Even if a forger of historical records were specially hired, the fact would still remain that all the young people who had the chance turned up at the dance, which was held for two reasons:

On the one hand, for the theology graduates to raise funds to go off abroad and visit holy sites, and on the other hand – at the end of the journey – for them to import one of those elderly theologians who were travelling the world at that time, and try, in meeting halls and at outdoor gatherings, to provide empirical evidence for the miracles of Christ.

But neither happened.

Neither did an elderly man appear with suitcases packed with miracles, nor was any of the young clergymen seen to sail away on board a ship.

Instead they plunged body and soul into the fight for benefices and neither Daniel nor Sigrid knew what became of the profits since they were so much in love that they forgot everything except the dance itself, which Sigrid, much later, is now recalling and remembers so clearly that a smile of ecstasy passes over her otherwise weary face.

The Theologians' Ball

At that moment she seems to stand up.

Younger and lighter.

Yes, so young and so light that she would prefer not to recognize the old woman sitting there reincarnated in the sofa several decades later, but standing in an enormous queue, which slowly but surely slips through the arched doorway to the marbled dance hall, outside which the cool breeze of a spring evening plays and the verses of the city's young poets glide bearing love like a country boy bowing in his Sunday best.

While she was buying a ticket in the foyer and paying for it with a laconic expression, Sigrid saw where the young theology graduates had lined up at the cloakroom at the end of a long corridor.

At first Sigrid thought, either in her childlike innocence or because they were all wearing tails and bow ties, that it was the dance-hall barmen all standing there, and if they were not barmen then they must surely be a peculiarly youthful and well-dressed male-voice choir.

And shortly afterwards, as she walked past them, Sigrid immediately noticed Daniel who, although she says so herself, was by far the most splendid of all the young theology graduates.

Yes, much more splendid than the prospective suffragan bishop, the cathedral deacon and the Free Church minister, and also the one in the middle who would later be convicted of embezzlement and tax evasion, and the one beside him who within a very few years would toss his cassock into the sea and turn up waving a red flag at other types of religious services and protest meetings.

Although smallest of the group and in that sense the most barmanly in appearance, there was something holy about Daniel which she saw immediately; as if all the sensitivity of the world were flowing beneath his skin.

So he captured her attention at once.

And it must have been mutual, for after the chain dance, when she had had to take a diagonal course across the floor to end up with him, they glided across the floor and even danced together in gentle contact long after the music had fallen silent in the interval, and, Daniel would confide to her later when they were married, a little tipsy from the communion wine, that it had probably been the intimate waltzes at the theologians' ball that released the tumultuous blood of hymn-writing into his veins; and anyone who cares to thumb through a hymn book can see that his earliest hymns are indeed dated from the night that the ball ended.

Nor is it any secret that immediately after the dance they began dating and Sigrid recalls their long, dignified walks along flagstoned pavements, furtive glances over cups of coffee and something no one saw in the park, right up until the day that Daniel plucked up his courage, cleared his throat and delivered his proposal of marriage, with both such a clerical tone of voice and so hymnwriterly an expression on his face that under these circumstances the word 'no' would surely have sounded like an outrageous act of blasphemy.

Yet, although in deference to the feminine custom she kept him waiting several days for her reply, there was no refusal in Sigrid's mind and the courage implied by her decision to say 'yes' was in full accordance with the heat of their love, for despite the prospect of coming top in both the Latin and French matriculation exams the next year, she followed unhesitatingly in Daniel's footsteps when he plunged into the battle for a benefice the moment their engagement was announced, pored over announcements of vacant parishes and read all the newspaper advertisements that the Ministry of Ecclesiastical Affairs published, and was even entertaining hopes of a job at the cemetery administration office when the call arrived and he was awarded a benefice in a remote village in the countryside.

Time Between the Mountains

Sigrid recalls the coach journey there so clearly:

How, young and in love, they had bumped along the pitted roads between mountains that stood waiting shrouded in fog the moment that the roads behind them disappeared, as if to underline that there would be no turning back.

And the darkness.

The darkness that came with the autumn.

It lay like a black puddle in the sky and remained there for months on end while the winter passed in sunless gloom under the dramatic mountains until the sun popped back up.

At first the beams were seen dancing on the peaks of the mountains and lighting up the expanses of snow upon them, and the sun was regarded as something so grand that it was welcomed with pancakes.

But that was not all, for the sun, the pancakes and the brightness that arrived, all were accompanied by the village singing in a choir that, kindled with a drop of the hard stuff, could sometimes be so frenzied that avalanches broke loose in the mountains and mudslides cascaded down their slopes.

So that even when the summer arrived the roads remained blocked, and because the telephone wires were continually snapping the outside world would sometimes completely forget that the village existed at all.

Sometimes money disappeared from circulation and various other laws were revoked, and in the meantime debts were simply worked out mentally and settled later when the co-operative society and the bank re-established contact with that much vaunted outside world.

And since the days, locked up within themselves, were often so similar to each other, long periods would pass when no one saw any reason to turn over the calendar and find out how time was getting along.

So it should not come as any surprise that Sigrid, on the coach, was looking forward in a certain sense to reading what remained of her grammar-school courses on an extra-mural basis in the privacy of the village and, at least, to gaining a thorough knowledge of Latin and French.

No, it is not really strange in the least that she was taken aback to find that, after all was said and done, this privacy turned out to be highly varied and colourful, and the life in the village such that, in order for its grammar, conjunctions and cases to be understood, all textbooks from the outside world would need both to fade and to be forgotten.

Or in other words: both the drama of the mountains and the sunless gloom of the winter, loneliness, claustrophobia and depression, these were all much stricter teachers than those who stood smartly at the blackboards of the city.

At first she felt the houses were squeaking like mice in the wind and she saw the local people only on the odd occasion when they passed by as she was looking out of the parlour window of the vicarage, which was on a hill overlooking the village.

To begin with, church attendance was nothing to write home about either.

Apart from funerals, which everyone attended when a fishing boat sank or someone died from mysterious causes, it hardly mattered in the least what day or at what time the church bells were rung; the congregation in the church always comprised the same people.

Besides Sigrid, the young vicar's wife, who always sat alone in the front pew watching her husband conducting the service, four teetotallers sat a few pews behind, all half-brothers who had all got religion after such prolonged and wild drinking bouts that it was anyone's guess if they would ever sober up again, still staggering and hiccuping when they spoke.

And one of the two village idiots, the one who customarily went around with a washing-bowl on his head, he always turned up, too, and was sometimes allowed to ring the church bells for Daniel, and sometimes the leader of the parish council came and the manager of the co-op with him, but they turned up only if Daniel promised to play whist with them at the end of service.

And then of course there is no forgetting the church choir, composed of eight housewives who were often weak of voice and hoarse owing to the large amount of their time they spent shouting at disobedient children.

But lack of voice was not the worst thing about their singing, for they knew only the hymns that Daniel's predecessor in the benefice had composed during the last years of his life, such appalling waffle, nonsense and rubbish, even sporadic sexual fantasies and blasphemy, that the Reverend Daniel felt it almost in breach of the laws of the church to allow their performance.

Which is why.

Although the hymns always reminded him of the theologians' ball and the intimate contact of the waltzes, the Reverend Daniel was prompted to seize his pen with all the more determination and vigour and double his output of poetry and hymns.

And it was then that he began – initially because of how bored Sigrid was – what would later prove to be a productive arrangement.

While Daniel warbled into the blue searching for melodies that fitted the verses, which he also frequently improvised as he was composing, Sigrid sat accompanying him on the organ and sometimes took part in creating the hymns and moreover even composed, without it ever being mentioned, some of their melodies.

No, in all the sheet music and hymn books that have been printed there is nowhere mention of anything but the fact that the Reverend Daniel composed all the hymns by himself.

But be that as it may, hymnody is mentioned here only because participation in the creation of hymns sufficed completely for the life of the congregation to begin flowing through Sigrid's veins, for she never insisted on being designated their author and it never even occurred to her that she had written the ones she had written.

But when the life of the congregation had come to her in this way, all her boredom was banished by sitting alone in the front pew and she started smiling at the teetotallers and playing with the village idiot at the same time as her contemplations of the matriculation cap to all intents and purposes vanished and she accepted that oblivion would swallow most grammatical rules of Latin and French provenance. Instead, she began organizing the life of the congregation with similar vigour to that with which Daniel composed both sermons and hymns.

So she put the church choir through training and established a Christian song and drama group with children and senior citizens and resurrected the Women's League which had petered out in the time of the previous vicar, because he was not only a bachelor but also so lurid and lecherous that no woman could stay in his presence for more than five minutes, and its resurrection brought cake sales, whist drives and accordion recitals, all that is considered the foundation of a flourishing religious life; and it was indeed in connection with the whist drives that Daniel's indefatigable interest in games of patience was born, which is mentioned so that no one should think it was the leader of the parish council and the manager of the co-op who inveigled this into him.

And the fish came and went and the mountain roads were either open or blocked and the years that Sigrid had felt at first would never pass had suddenly become ten when the Reverend Daniel began once more to apply for benefices, this time in the city where his thoughts tended, partly because he wanted to read lessons on the radio and write in the papers and hear what was going on within the rapidly growing profession of clergymen, for as far as Daniel could make out there were churches and bank branches being built on virtually every street corner in the city which must surely mean that not only finance was flourishing there, but also religion in a similar fashion.

In all, Daniel's applications for benefices in the city would amount to seventy-four, both because of the large number of applicants there always were for benefices in the city and also because of the few people who longed to move to his remote village to take his place. So the years in the village between the mountains became ten more or twenty in all when . . .

Yes, one sunny day Sigrid saw Daniel out of the parlour window of the vicarage on the hill, running at full pelt along the main street of the village.

Of Toffees and Churches

With one hand he was throwing toffees over a group of children who were running after him in a line dragging wooden cars behind them on pieces of string and rattling wrenches, and in the other he was waving an envelope marked, in the front bottom corner, the Ministry of Ecclesiastical Affairs, inside which is a letter that, after reading it at the post office, had occasioned the Reverend Daniel to buy toffees for the children.

Signed by both the Bishop and the Minister for Ecclesiastical Affairs, the letter states that it is in confirmation of the fact that the national authorities, secular and spiritual, accept his application and hereby accede to his request, and that from the beginning of the next month he can take over the parish that is on the way to becoming the largest and most populous not only in the city, but also thereby in the whole country.

Once again the coach bounced between the mountains, along the same bumpy road as twenty years previously, only in the opposite direction, and Sigrid, who had felt then that she was driving into the darkness, she was almost disconsolate and immediately began to recall the village with a warmth that conjured forth sunbeams, pancakes, the singing of choirs and daylight.

Beside her sat Daniel, who was not thinking of the village but rather trying to imagine from the letter what the congregation was like, toying moreover with the notion that the office of park-keeper might belong to it as a supplementary duty, and yearning so much to see the church and the vicarage where they would live that once they reached town he could hardly wait for the coach to stop, but ordered a cab immediately to take them to where their expectations lay.

But what disappointment; and on arriving he understood for the first time the grin that had played across the taxi-driver's lips, for the church he intended to examine and had mentally outlined over and again . . .

Yes, ten out of ten, the building work was not even under way, and likewise its large and numerous congregation existed only in the form of unfinished foundations of houses.

The sole explanation the Reverend Daniel received about this state of affairs from the bishop's office and other ecclesiastical authorities was that the letter that had been sent to him at the village, such a long distance between the mountains, had clearly set off a year earlier than planned.

And so it turned out that for a whole year the Reverend Daniel was on the street without a benefice and the couple had to rent accommodation in town while the church was being built and the vicarage put in order, and in order to hurry the work along the Reverend Daniel turned up every morning in a boilersuit, along with all the carpenters and plasterers and other building workers.

Sometimes they could use him for simple tasks and running errands. He stripped nails from planks, planed timber and went off to fetch fizzy drinks, cakes and sweets for them, even collected drink for them from the off-licence and was both healthy-looking and weather-beaten when they were finally able to move into the vicarage, around the same time that the huge fifteen-storey apartment blocks were beginning to acquire a new shape.

By then the foundations had also turned into four-storey houses and the council blocks and trade-union blocks were appearing, along with detached houses that sprouted like mushrooms out of the hills above the valley where the farm on the other side of the park still stands, this evening so much later.

Churchwardenship and Cleaning

Because of how new everything was, the people, the houses and the cars, everything being born and coming into being, it is obvious that during Daniel's initial period as a shepherd of souls on the estate there was not much in the way of funerals.

As if no one there had the time to die, because everything was so young and new.

However, babies were baptized, teenagers confirmed and adults came to get both married and divorced. To begin with, of course, there were more who got married, but the divorces increased afterwards.

But while it prevailed that weddings and marriages flourished, some weeks there were so many children to baptize that it was no surprise if the Reverend Daniel happened on occasion to get their names mixed up.

Worse, later on, was the single week when so many people died that he mixed up a number of his funeral speeches, nor was everyone impressed by Daniel's stunt of inviting people to call on him and have a hand in writing their own funeral speeches.

For the most part, however, this remained only an idea, and it is not known that many people took advantage of this service, which was certainly not available during the swaddling years of the congregation here described.

But the construction work.

Not only was it conducted with such haste that the installation of central heating in the walls of the children's chapel was completely forgotten, but was also halted long before it was completed, and the outside of the church was left unplastered apart from a few splashes of concrete on the nave.

Some people attribute this simply to the customary lack of funds, while others maintain that the ecclesiastical authorities and even the bishop himself had found fault with the Reverend Daniel, both because of how readily he declared the supplementary income of his spiritual work to the tax authorities, and also because shortly after receiving the keys to the church, yes when he turned once again to composing hymns, he also began writing pop songs.

His acquaintance with pop songs derived in all likelihood from the large number he had heard on the American Forces Radio while working on building the church, and is nowhere said to have impaired the quality of his hymns; on the contrary, Daniel's best ones date from the same time that he was writing pop songs.

What irritated the ecclesiastical authorities above all about Daniel's pop songs was that they were so sentimental and slow that they were always waltzed to when played in dance halls, and also the performers with whom Daniel seemed to consider his compositions had affinities, a silk-clad rock band comprising three ginger-haired brass-players and a vocalist who was a policeman by day and is said to have swung the microphone exactly as he did his truncheon when conducting traffic.

Besides the above, the group consisted of a guitarist, a bass-player and a drummer, but the rumour that spread like a haunting ghost through the church synods, that the Reverend Daniel sometimes played mouth organ with them, had no grounds in fact.

Be that as it may, after all his navvying, acting as builder's mate and stripping nails and running errands, the Reverend Daniel was not only fully acquainted with the pop music of the day, but also so accustomed to all manner of secular chores and tasks that he felt it out of the question to appoint a special churchwarden or employ a cleaning lady.

No, he preferred to see central heating installed in the children's chapel along with more of whatever else was lacking, so the church-wardenship fell to his lot, while the cleaning was in Sigrid's hands, except when she was helped by girls from confirmation classes, or the pre-school children, neither of which happened often.

Therefore it is not so wild an assumption that when, on the dark-brown sofa, she came to her senses once more in the manner described above, with a piercing sting, common or garden ache, or rheumatism . . .

No, it is not so wild an assumption that in her mind she is hunched over a plastic bucket with a cloth and mop, looking with tired eyes over the floor by the church door.

Fire Fire

Sigrid takes a look around the parlour.

First she gives a sideways glance at Daniel who, seemingly immutable, is as engrossed as ever.

Then she looks down at the embroidery, which is still lying unmoved on the carpet, bathing in the beams of light that pour on to it.

Perhaps she should pull herself together and pick up where she left off.

It is not a worthy way to meet one's maker over a single piece of embroidery.

Such a long time since she wanted to finish it and take it along to show the Women's League.

Weren't they talking about exhibiting it at the fête?

Sigrid reaches out for the sewing needle on the edge of the sofa, looks whether there is still blood on the point, then leans forward, feels her forehead growing hotter and her joints cracking and drops the embroidery twice before she manages to take a firm hold of it between her fingers.

Slumps back in the sofa, heaves a sigh and puffs.

It is this lethargy that descends upon me from time to time, fatigue that wakes in my eyes like a lighthouse-keeper, fear that grows like an embryo within my womb.

Perhaps Daniel is right and it's just vitamin deficiency?

I can scarcely manage to lift my shopping bag and for months I have been unable to play on the organ for the pre-school children without fainting on to the keyboard, to say nothing of being able to do handicraft with them.

My hands feel like taxidermized birds, my feet like anaesthetized horses.

While she contemplates the embroidery, half of Jesus Christ's face is in front of her, tender but sad.

As if she could feel the expression herself.

She longs to hold Jesus up against the light and show Daniel, but does not want to disturb him because she knows he must finish the homework. The children are waiting excitedly to see it and Daniel needs to turn to other more important tasks.

But what Sigrid dislikes most is the fact that now he needs to wash the floor by the church door himself and go out to ring the bells no matter what the weather.

The needle passes through the embroidery, Jesus's hair grows and his cheeks fill out.

The right eye will prove difficult.

Beams of light are reflected in the needle.

Sometimes they rebound in her eyes, causing her to fumble, blinding her, and she has undone the eye three times and made two different noses when she gives up and lays the embroidery in her lap and drops her hands holding the sewing needle over the edge of the sofa.

Fire fire . . .

Somewhere inside her head a dream seems to burn, as if kindling her mind and crackling with sparks in the sofa, inside her head as it leans and rolls on to her right shoulder then forward as her eyes close.

Her hair falls in a black tumble over her face.

Dream with the Barking of Dogs

As if in obedience to some supernatural harmony in the universe, an internal clock or rhythmical drum in the innards of the souls, at precisely the same moment that Sigrid nods and falls asleep on the sofa, the singing has passed its climax and everything has fallen into total silence in the saddlemaker's workshop.

Like the stuffed fox heads, the whale skeleton and ornaments; matching the furniture, the fishermen lie there, some having rolled out of their saddles, others off the workbenches, and the saddlemaker himself is stooped forward.

He has stopped declaiming and instead of singing heroic couplets his head mumbles lullabies in a sorrowful voice.

He leans back in his story-teller's chair and gives a hiccup that causes the gold-plated bell on his waistcoat to ring, and in his arms he is holding a herring barrel containing homebrewed ale.

Between verses he turns on the tap, opens his mouth and lets the homebrewed ale pour straight into his stomach.

His heart pounds and his face is red and hot.

But while the saddlemaker is sitting there and the fishermen are lying with the saddle fixed between two fox heads, farmer Gunnar, in the same position he has been all the time, is asleep upright.

So deep and alcoholic is his sleep that he could hardly dare to dream of ever being able to remember the dream he is dreaming now.

This dream:

When the mermaids who appeared on the gutter of the roof earlier that evening come to him with flowing locks and red lips he sees suns, countless suns, holding hands and moving as if dancing an elfin dance and wearing red tasselled caps above his farm in the valley and the tasselled caps are beams of light, so clear and bright that all the shadows that have ever been can be seen packing their bags and disappearing in one of those new-fangled jet planes.

Then the weeds and chickweed flee and potatoes the size of footballs grow up out of his pockets as he stands in the farmyard looking eastwards when the ornamental plants suddenly burst out through the frame of the greenhouse in the park and the trees grow to reach in an instant the size of the giants that the saddlemaker says live in ancient sagas and are still found in the west fjords.

And in a single instant the trees grow over the windows of the detached houses and surround the valley where the grass has mutated so that every blade has the precisely calculated circumference of one elephant's trunk and some of the children who come running down into the valley from the quarter have tractors under the soles of their shoes and the cows, many of which speak more than six languages, milk so furiously that all over the fields and into the ditches flow rivers of milky white.

Naked on top of stones, the mermaids sit and govern the courses of the rivers, and farmer Gunnar, feeling he needs to have a few words with them about the male–female communications infrastructure, has set off with his genitalia rampant when his black dog suddenly begins to bark.

He looks around in the dream but the dog is nowhere to be seen, he can only hear it louder, louder . . .

Heels and Needles

Death Around the Night

Of the Journeys of the Darkness: A Few Remarks Regarding Local Landmarks and Nationality

Snores pass through the night and outside, while a black dog is barking, either with its eyes open or in the dream of a man who sleeps standing up, the darkness hovers outside with pure silver raindrops in its arms.

It hovers in pitch-black particles up in the sky, over the roofs, the lamp-posts and trees, around gardens, streets and fields, hovers where the day vanished from the sky to allow the evening to come and travel around the night.

Around death, the raindrops and the night.

Alarm clocks tick on bedside tables inside the houses, and beside the bedside tables human faces are arranged in such numerous permutations along the heads of beds that it is understandably rather strange for you who pass through this night in oilskins to see all those sleeping people.

Is there really only one clergyman up and about?

And what is one clergyman in the darkness of a whole estate?

Yes, look there, inside the workshop.

Around the saddles, about the workbenches, lies a complete party and with his herring barrel in his arms a bloated-faced man is beginning to snore.

Or all those children.

Why should they always emit sporadic laughter as if someone is tickling them or prickling their nerves in the darkness behind their eyes?

Or the woman with her head slumped forward with half of Jesus Christ's face embroidered and a sewing needle under her fingers on the edge of the sofa.

Or . . .

Yes, as you can see, there is also a first-rate barbershop here, a large white school and a shop with both an ice-cream machine and a pot full of hot-dogs.

And women.

Plenty of hospitable women.

Some of them so used to someone turning up late in the evening that they even open the door without looking to see who it is.

So to speak.

As you can see and hear.

It is quite out of the question that those who have turned the night into their vehicle need guidance or other signs.

Far from it.

Most of the local landmarks look quite obvious.

For there is also much to justify and suggest that someone, some two or more, among the deceased fishermen who earlier that evening were seen to die in violent waves and now roam with their features in torn oilskins . . .

Roam the estate, roam the streets and roam the darkness in the estate.

Yes, there is much to suggest that these are familiar men who, wise to the world, find their way around both houses and apartment blocks.

Judging from all the signs this is scarcely a foreign ship's crew, scarcely people who believe they are somewhere other than they actually are.

No.

These are clearly not exotic creatures.

Rather . . .

Yes, who knows . . .

Perhaps spirits, flickering beings, officially domiciled in some of the flats of the houses or blocks.

So why do they cause such a stir?

Why do they seem to wreak havoc across the night?

Is their wrath perhaps only righteous indignation at the fate they met when even help itself was beyond help?

Or might they have no control over the form they have assumed?

Of Easy and Loose Women

No matter where.

In the darkened flats, in benighted houses and dim blocks alike, everywhere women with a reputation for easy and loose living of various sorts are running for all they are worth.

In all innocence they have opened their doors or lifted the latch and, as if nothing could be more natural, drawn back the bolts of their doors.

Or even said 'come in', then turned around with some ancient or new lover in mind who has turned up carrying the loneliness of the night in his baggage.

Except.

Instead of warm hands, they have been suddenly seized by ice-cold briny fingers that run down their necks or grip their shoulders and in an instant white brassières have turned into falling bird's wings and transparent négligés have been metamorphosed into tattered rags.

Screaming in terror, the women of easy virtue have been forced to flee with their naked breasts bobbing in front of them and their bloody hearts jumping inside them.

So fast, so fast, that in darkened hallway mirrors they have only just managed to catch a glance of oilskins.

They have been startled by men so curiously cold and blue in the face.

Between the corners of rooms with sofas in, through kitchens, bathrooms and hallways, the chase has gone on everywhere:

In and out of wardrobes and cupboards.

Up and down in the lifts.

Even into the laundry rooms and storerooms.

And wherever the women flee to.

Thumping and plodding, in wet oilskins and waders, everywhere like films that develop in your eyes, everywhere the fishermen appear.

And some are so lustful, so vehement and lustful, that despite the cold that surrounds them they drop their rubber trousers and take off their oilskins before they get the women underneath them or in their arms.

In their hands they wave giant penises which, as thick as a bottle and the length of a hammer's shaft, with veins standing out like inflated motorways, are all covered in goosepimples.

In some places curtains are whisked down from windows and, bringing radios and flowerpots with them, are dashed over carpets until the inevitable moment when everything resounds as if chests the size of whales are rippling back and forth across the ocean, at the same time as tortured screams drown in laughter so gigantic that the neighbours of the women of easy virtue can only conclude they are just throwing another party.

So it is no surprise when the banging returns with the screams, but this time with footsteps whose sound resembles, if not tables being turned over during marital squabbles, then the beating of hoofs or a sledgehammer being struck at bullhides stretched tight for a drum.

In Which Reference Is Made, Among Other Things, to a Barber's Pole, a Pulpit and a Man Who Sleeps with His False Teeth in a Glass of Water

But it is not only women with a reputation for easy virtue and loose living who have suffered unexpected visits.

No.

Someone has also stood on the gravel outside the barbershop and knocked on Anton the barber's windows with such force that for all his sweet dreams he has started up three times and leapt out of his red-covered spring bed, put on his slippers and gone outside without seeing a thing there but the darkness.

The night, the raindrops and the darkness.

All that hovers around the jangling barber's pole.

And noise has been heard, commotion has been heard.

Someone has padded and plodded along the corridors of the white school and the cowbell belonging to Frimann the caretaker used to call the classes in for assembly has been rung so loud and piercingly that some neighbouring children have even set off for school, somnambulant in their pyjamas.

Maps have atomized; globes have vanished.

And someone must have taken Herbert the headmaster's pulpit and put it in the broom cupboard where the cleaning ladies keep their things, for surely Herbert does not intend to stand in there the next time he addresses the school.

Likewise, spare parts and tools have disappeared from garages, chequered thermos flasks have vanished from the windows of creosoted worksheds and Sunday dinners have been removed from refrigerators.

And here in the twilight . . .

In the dark twilight, under the falling raindrops of the night.

Isn't that the hatch of Siggi's shop wide open?

Oh yes.

Someone must have kicked in the door and removed the glass that usually covers the crossword magazines, yellow pop-fan magazines and true-love stories for men only.

Yes, the same intruder has clearly done that while breaking down the hatch.

For inside the shop.

Neither on its dappled floor nor the darkness of its white shelves.

Wherever you care to look.

Not a sign of beer bottles, pipe tobacco nor cigarettes.

Besides which the hot-dog pot has been plugged in and the

ice-cream machine is working away and thick ice-cream is leaking in long strips down on to the floor.

At the same time.

In a flat behind the shop.

By the side of a man who has laid his blue brass-band uniform, folded, across the back of a chair, Siggi is asleep while the ice-cream leaks and the hot-dogs boil.

He is wearing loud pyjamas and his mouth is wide open, and while the darkness rises out of his black gullet his huge, smiling false teeth await the call of duty in a glass of water standing on a bedside table by the side of the head of the bed.

Cables in the Raindrops

And outside, the darkness floats.

It floats out of the gullet of the sky.

Pours from silent lips out into the almighty.

No white clouds like the false teeth in the glass.

Follows the courses of thin streams along the streets, looping and curling one after the other around the fishermen's feet as they roam about as cold as corpses in their oilskins, blue-headed in a fatigued trance.

Roam between houses, around the night; death, the raindrops and the night.

No, it is not until the church bells come into sight, not until their eyes notice the ponderous bells with their ropes hanging down in the raindrops, yes only then do the fishermen first stop to contemplate from a distance the legally sanctioned holy shrine of the estate, the Reverend Daniel's parish church.

Perhaps one of them knows Daniel or they have heard of him like everyone else who listens to the radio, heard his hymns being sung or remember his old pop songs from the days of groups in silk suits.

Over their torn green oilskins, pure silver raindrops fall, playing about their eyes like sad tears, and somewhere in the distance of the darkness the wind seems to reach out for a shiny polished flute.

First it places it to the drenched lips of the universe, then fills its lungs with air and does a few inaudible breathing exercises.

At least, the two church bells stand as still as the grave, do not budge, and the ropes that the local children sometimes sneak up to swing on, they are rustling so minutely that their movement can hardly be discerned with the naked eye.

Meanwhile, the church floats in gloomy darkness and, shut tight, echoes only the raindrops, the falling raindrops as they beat upon the creosoted roof and the windows, upon the blue-lit cross which, helpless and lonely, stares out into the darkness, out into the night, the raindrops and the darkness.

Dynamically Busy

Several Paths to Choose From

If you, dear reader, put yourself for a moment in the shoes of the deceased ship's crew and look, as they did, straight ahead at the parish church with its blue-lit cross.

What do you see right in front of your eyes, but exactly what the crew sees: namely a firmly locked door along with the darkness floating in the window.

So the question surely arises whether anyone lives here who can afford to identify himself as the Lord God Almighty or whether the darkness is just darkness, pitch-black particles of nothing.

But as you know.

When the path to holiness proves unnegotiable, there are often other, more mundane paths, for a single unnegotiable path: doesn't that show that there are least three others?

For this reason it is also right to point out that to the left, northwards, facing the mountains with their snow-white caps in the distance, lies the path from the church over several hills and out to a large, crescent-shaped street.

This is the path you would take were you ever invited along to the saddlemaker's workshop for a drink, while beyond the crescent-shaped street rise the houses overlooking the bay.

The path to the left is therefore also the path taken to reach the mental hospital and likewise the sea where the ship of the deceased crew lies like a beached whale on the shore.

You can also turn around and walk away from the church down a small slope that leads to a row of shops and an asphalted yard.

But when that is counted, only one main path remains.

The path that the Reverend Daniel walks every day, while to the right, a stone's throw from the church, along a paved walk through a field of clover, stands the vicarage, which comes into view along with the huge fifteen-storey apartment blocks that some people say are like gigantic trolls and others compare to birds of prey with electrified yellow eyes.

Behind the church, behind the vicarage and the apartment blocks, stand the old hills with their mysterious huge rocks, the bunker and the well.

Building work has been going on there of late. Headed by mechanical diggers and bulldozers, and also with navvies who pick with their axes and shovels, an attempt is being made to level out the hills to allow a car park to be built for the residents of the apartment blocks; and this development has by no means progressed without hitches.

But enough of that for the time being, for there is no avoiding . . .

Rustling in the Leaves

. . . neither this evening nor any other.

This night nor any other.

Over the sloping roof of the clerical residence, too, the raindrops are falling, and around the concrete walls, over the flowerbeds and knotty trees in the garden, the darkness hovers, flapping its raven-black wings.

Except that.

This evening and this night.

Yes, the difference between Daniel's vicarage and the houses and apartment blocks in its vicinity is that apart from sporadic lights in the little windows of bathrooms where someone is sitting with a stomach bug or some other sort of ailment, and excluding the handful of burning lights in the hallways of families who fear ghosts, the lights have been turned off everywhere and the windows are benighted in both the houses and the apartments, while the lights are still on and everything is lit up inside the vicarage.

And not without reason, for this evening and this night . . .

Even though Sigrid is sitting in her rose-patterned dress drooping her head on the sofa against the pedal organ, with half of Jesus

Christ's face embroidered in her lap and a sewing needle which, with her hand, she pushes over the edge and releases on to the floor, the Reverend Daniel is still up and has not gone to bed in the least.

On the contrary, he is sitting wide awake, with his shirtsleeves rolled up and his reading glasses on the end of his nose, at the round table, working with such unexampled vigour that his head seems to be an inexhaustible spring of spiritual energy or the coursing of the blood through his veins seems to be producing stimulants.

Unless both.

At least, the Reverend Daniel is concentrating so hard and is so engrossed in his work that he pays heed to neither the shadowy darkness of the heavens nor the clear silver dripping of the raindrops.

Even less does the rhythmical ticking of the clock in the parlour capture his mind, nor does it occur to him to look at his watch.

Nothing disturbs his dynamic quiet.

Not even the repressed heartbeat of Sigrid asleep on the sofa, nor the rustling outside, the rustling that constantly recurs and only causes Daniel to wonder how peculiarly the remaining leaves seem to rustle out there in the dark.

The Shepherd with His Crook

All the same, there is no denying that, in the lit room, Daniel's unflinching devotion and energy have produced such a fine day's work that there is a hint from his glowing expression, his reddened cheeks and eyes full of childlike glee, of a certain triumph shining forth when he turns over the last drawings in the pile and the last ducklings run through his mind as he recalls the classes where the pre-school children sat on hard old pews behind the swing doors to their chapel – which on account of lack of piping in the walls is heated with an antique electric radiator – drawing with yellow Pluto crayons at the long wooden table with its brown-painted planks, yes, each one drawing a duck through rustling tracing paper, then cutting them out and colouring and gluing them, along with yellow suns, white clouds and blue mountains, on to thick square sheets of paper, listening, while they did so, to Daniel describing all at once: Jesus, God, flowers, lambs and fishes.

And now the papers are lying on the table and the Reverend Daniel looks contentedly with a smiling, tearful expression of joy on his face, at the pile, the large pile beside the patience cards, and beside each duckling, each sun and each cloud and each mountain, he has written gentle, encouraging words, sometimes even whole passages from the Scriptures or hymns in full.

So there is no need to be surprised at the amount of time it took him to go over all the drawings, for if all the pre-school children who attend the chapel are added up, they amount according to Daniel's records to three hundred and fifty-six in total, thereof one hundred and eighty-four boys and one hundred and seventy-two girls.

Ah, the sweet little things, the sweet little things, the Reverend Daniel says out loud to himself as he closes his eyes with that peaceful expression of repose which within him conjures up his own image in the guise of a shepherd with a crook walking the moors and the children chasing him with lambs' heads and little tails wagging in the sun.

Wearing a long robe and using his hands as a trumpet, he calls out in a voice that echoes in the halls of the mountains, and is rushing to search for some children who have strayed away when the whishing, rustling leaves in his mind suddenly become thumping knocks.

Footsteps resound all over the house.

Someone seems to be fiddling with a screwdriver at the front door and at the very moment that roars of laughter sweep in through the letterbox, the doorbell rings.

Heels and Needles

Perils of the Soul under the Parlour Table

Boom boom boom.

His heart pounds.

Boom boom boom.

As the laughter fills the coat rack by the front door, tugs at the arm of a green poplin mackintosh and crawls into the thick pocket of an overcoat, someone seems to grip the handle of the front door and deliver a kick at its lower right-hand corner.

Boom boom boom.

It is not only the little lambs that disperse with bleating cries in all directions and tumble into the depths of the darkness, for all the suns are extinguished as well and in desperation the shepherd tosses away his crook, sheds his robe, and flees.

Boom boom boom.

Like a soap bubble, his peaceful expression of repose explodes into the air and with his heart leaping like a mouse the Reverend Daniel sits there, scared out of his wits, thinking as a spasm runs through him that sends his chair tumbling backwards and knocks his kneecap under the table: there are burglars here, robbers, even murderers.

Boom boom boom.

Admittedly, Daniel knows, he ought to be able to tell himself, he can think himself lucky at not having fallen over backwards and hit the back of his head on the windowsill, for then they could have come in and finished him off as he lay there unconscious with the back of his head covered in blood, his brain wobbling and rolling around like a wino on a never-ending binge.

But he says ouch, Daniel ouches a silent ouch, his face like a cat spitting, right on the verge of uttering a curse, when the roars of laughter return and pour over him like crime reports on the back pages of the newspapers.

Boom boom boom.

In a flash countless men wearing gloves appear to him, some carrying crowbars, others wearing knuckledusters and with rotten teeth.

Like air playing around an inflatable bed or his bones shrinking and turning to rubber.

This is how the Reverend Daniel feels his body pouring off the chair and oozing down under the table where he sits on all fours like a dog, trembling with his hair like the gnarled branches of a tree, wondering if it would not be wiser to hide behind the floor-length curtain, when he suddenly remembers his wallet in the pocket of his coat by the door.

The Battles of Alexander the Great

The banknotes, the wages of his public office in his wallet, seem to tug at his heart.

Should I let a bunch of rogues fleece me?

Is it my design to stand here like some humble beggar or coward, or should I rise up and confront those here present?

Should I or should I not?

In the midst of these ponderings, but without answering himself, the Reverend Daniel crawls from beneath the round parlour table and gets to his feet behind the door, switches off the lights, closes the door, and darts into the hallway.

The hallway stretches like a long tunnel and his heartbeat echoes while a cold gust of wind plays across his face and crawls down the neck of his shirt where he can feel his shivers tiptoeing as, trembling but with quiet dexterity, he manages to take hold of a carpetbeater hanging in the hallway opposite the mirror.

The mirror tugs at the darkness, drinking it as if from the neck of an invisible bottle, and the Reverend Daniel, who sneaks in with cat-like padding feet in his slippers, wields the carpetbeater, so convinced that someone is standing by the coat rack and rummaging in the coats that, without looking either to the left or the right, hurls himself through the door, takes a leap and jumps straight into the coat rack with the carpetbeater poised in the air like a club.

As he lands in the shoes without having grabbed any legs, Sigrid's green poplin mackintosh falls on top of him from its peg, and because Daniel cannot see anything for the cassock dangling on its peg right in front of his face, he thinks for a moment he is being attacked and wriggles his legs, waving the carpetbeater back and forth without anyone fighting back.

However, the front door is open and now, on the porch, the raindrops sound in his ears for the first time, beating while he looks out into the darkness at the dim houses, the church bells, the rope and the church itself, in its tightly shut darkness.

It rains over his shoulders on to his white nylon shirt and to find out what is going on he decides to walk a full circle around the house, naturally hoping and praying that none of the local residents is awake at a window to see him prowling around with a carpetbeater in the middle of the night, for that would be news worth telling and would spread like lightning from one person to the next.

First he looks over the clover field, then into the dustbin yard and between the gnarled trees behind the house, but finds nothing except a few bottles and three crumpled cigarette packets lying together with countless leaves on the ground.

Beyond the garden, cars are standing and waiting in tranquil silence for the morning when the residents of the apartment blocks wake up.

Nothing else.

Only an fruitless quest, soaked shoulders from the rain and a sense of excitement that leave the Reverend Daniel, once he has closed the front door behind him and hung the carpetbeater back up in its place, quite the opposite of sleepy after turning on the wall-light by the round table in the parlour once again.

At first he is wondering whether he ought to return his fantasy about children or even write a hymn, but then, as if the Lord God Almighty had pointed them out to him, his eye falls upon the patience cards lying in the shadow of the pile of papers on the table.

What a merciful gift!

Such repose of the soul that a game of patience always brings flows across him like water in a swimming pool, so that everything, no matter what, drowns in forgetfulness, in the oblivion where the battles of Alexander the Great are fought.

Even forgetfulness forgets itself too the moment that the sense of time is cast to the winds.

An Intuition in the Dark

For this reason it is not easy to say how many games of patience the Reverend Daniel has played or how long he has been sitting there doing battle with hearts, spades, diamonds and clubs when a light yawn crosses his face.

Like a tranquil harp, his repose of soul closes his eyes again, and while his consciousness steps out of oblivion and awakens at the round parlour table, it can be discerned from the movement of his lips that the Reverend Daniel is praying.

Amen and he stands up, puts the cards into the pack, nods his head to the pile of papers with ducklings on them, places his reading glasses in their case and takes off his slippers, leaving them footless under the table.

Shortly afterwards he is back in the hallway, having turned off the lights, and the darkness hovers completely devoid of burglars and with no crowbars about his head, and he is perfectly collected and absorbed in his thoughts when, at the mirror facing the carpetbeater, he feels an intuition that he has forgotten something.

But as so often when an intuition comes, what it is that he has forgotten the Reverend Daniel simply cannot remember.

No, not a clue, and he checks whether the electrical appliances in the kitchen are in order, checks twice whether the lights are turned off, and convinces himself there are no burning candles about and, what on earth!, he thinks the elves and dwarfs on the hill are playing tricks on him like the time long ago when they were always ringing his doorbell and chasing him and pinching him in the testicles.

But no . . .

He is so completely stumped that nothing occurs to him except what the man in the grey coat said to him the other day when he came to mend the organ, the pedal organ that had gone so false the hymns were sounding unrhymed and avant-garde or like arias completely disconnected from their original form, when the tuner said that to keep the organ in good shape, since it was a good organ, it was worth the effort, many times over, to close the lid over the keyboard, otherwise dust would settle on the keys and they would get dirty and go yellow, for the lid is a similar kind of cover to the organ as the lips are to the teeth.

With this useful advice in mind the Reverend Daniel turns around and walks into the parlour without turning on the lights, heads straight for the organ with his fingertips, his fingers outstretched towards the lid, when he encounters something; something sharp, pointed, piercing, naked and painful.

In an instant the room is filled with screams, and hopping on one foot the Reverend Daniel howls over the sofa where Sigrid is asleep with her embroidery in her lap and one hand on the edge of the sofa, and then he sees, remembers and understands, that it was of course her that he had forgotten or more correctly not remembered or he had thought she had gone to bed or . . .

The pain leaves him no time to speculate, no chance to think things over, for the blood seeping out of his heel colours the carpet red and the sharp needle seems to have penetrated completely vertically and disappeared at full length inside his heel and Daniel feels it thrusting forth like a spear when Sigrid wakes up.

She does not know what to think, if he has gone mad and started playing Cowboys and Indians in the middle of the night in the parlour, so startled, absolutely, downright startled, that she even thinks she is still dreaming when she realizes, with the natural consequence that the dream she was actually dreaming fades away into nothingness, all of it except some curious fiery-yellow figures around the organ.

A little later, with a little washing-bowl full of lukewarm water, Sigrid kneels at his feet, takes off his bloody sock and, using a pair of stamp tweezers, manages to pinch the silver-plated end of the sewing needle and draw it out before cleansing the wound by wetting it with saliva and rubbing her fingertips across it.

She waits until the bleeding stops, first cleans the cut with soap and ethanol, then applies antiseptic cream and wraps it in a white bandage held in place by fawn plasters to allow the wound to heal.

Next she supports the whining and limping Daniel off to bed, sits him down on the edge and helps him undress, turns off the lights and spreads the quilt over him.

She makes no attempt to comprehend the disjointed words pouring out of his mouth, just kisses him goodnight, with her own thoughts behind the darkness that pours forth as if emptied out of a bucket over her head.

Heads in Hats

Ding dong ding dong ding dong.

Ding dong ding dong ding dong.

Ding dong ding dong ding . . .

Whether the Reverend Daniel is asleep behind his closed eyes or whether in the twilight of pain he is just lying between sleep and the waking state.

It is not easy to tell.

Since he is not even aware himself, he could quite easily be wide awake when all this ding-donging fills the darkness and the church bells start ringing so clearly.

He mentally rules out for a start that some young pranksters are swinging on the ropes at this time of night, or that some unfortunate wino, intending to hang himself, has failed so dismally.

But whatever it is, under all circumstances the Reverend Daniel wants to know what is going on and not just wants but knows it is his duty to make sure unauthorized persons do not take liberties with consecrated bells.

For this reason he sits up and gets out of bed, but when he does so and when he gets dressed in his sleep behind closed eyes, in a dream or in the delirium of pain in the twilight between sleep and the waking state; this is not clear to him, only that the darkness is dark and he is dragging his foot.

But the raindrops falling on the porch are exactly the same as when he had been standing there with the carpetbeater.

One by one the steps pass under his soles and the paved path carries his feet over the clover field, on to the gravel in front of the church where there is nothing noticeable about the bells except that the clappers, although still swinging gently, have long since stopped striking the chambers.

On the other hand, the tightly shut church door is wide open, its darkness illuminated, and the sound of an organ can be heard as if at midnight mass. Inquisitive as a departed soul, Daniel passes through the doors and the first thing he knows is that he is standing in the porch when the music stops.

All over the floor are footprints and little wet puddles lie everywhere, but wherever Daniel looks, in the cupboard, the toilet and everywhere, he cannot see a soul.

So he opens the broom cupboard, takes the plastic bucket, mop and floorcloth and the next few minutes pass like the arc-like swinging of a man tossing and turning and continually nudging with his elbows, until the puddles have disappeared and the footprints as if they had never been trodden.

The Reverend Daniel has turned off the lights and is locking the church and trying the door handle to make sure it is definitely locked, then turns around to limp away when his heart seizes and his eyes stop dead.

It is like a gust of wind moving across the nape of his neck or the world filling up with weird phenomena; he not only hears the laughter he had heard through the letterbox while he was a shepherd strolling around with his sheep, but also sees a crowd of men standing beneath the church bells, all wearing torn green oilskins and waders, so curiously pallid that the Reverend Daniel immediately concludes they have been on a long binge and needed to throw up frequently.

What he fails to understand, however, is why they did not take off their oilskins before getting drunk, because he never drinks wearing his cassock and he is about to reprimand them, bellow at them in thunderous tones and preach about disorderly behaviour at night.

But then the fishermen raise their arms and the Reverend Daniel, thinking they are about to say something and are asking permission to speak, moves closer to hear what they are going to say.

But instead of talking the fishermen are silent, surrounded by a quietness as silent as the grave, and the Reverend Daniel is wondering what all these arms are supposed to represent when oh yes, they are going to take off their hats, for now they are putting their hands on the brims of their sou'westers.

And Daniel, as if to present them with something in return, fishes a crucifix out of his jacket pocket as they tug at their brims, but not only take off their hats to bow but their heads with them as if stuck on, and the moment that the Reverend Daniel faints on the gravel by the belltower outside the church they vaporize and vanish, and a light goes on in the vicarage bedroom.

Part III

Epilogue of the Raindrops

Black Banks of Cloud

Closed for the Summer Holidays

Of Little White Meteorological Stations

The days pass.

The nights pass.

And to start with, in the beginning, is that business with the weather reports, the weather and the weather reports, but long before they rush off with countless invisible postmen along the proverbial waves of ether, and long before they become a human voice flowing with monotonous timbre out of radio sets; yes, it is such common knowledge as scarcely to need mentioning, that weather reports are first taken out of little white meteorological stations that are almost an exact replica of precisely those famous bird-houses that can boast of having been used in the manufacture of certain types of clock called, obviously enough, cuckoo clocks, which say 'cuckoo' like a singing teacher practising a birdsong with children.

And in this way the little white meteorological stations bear little relation to other types of bird-houses, neither pigeon coops, chicken runs nor parrot cages, even less certain varieties of nest.

For of course there are no birds inside them; neither clairvoyant ravens nor eagles nor gyrfalcons, to say nothing of gaolbirds, dolly birds or parrots hermetically sealed with the instincts of weather-wise farmers.

Instead there are only a few instruments to be seen, devised and manufactured by scientists after centuries of research into the innards of the atmosphere to allow the state of the heavens to be revealed in similar fashion to a thermometer that reveals the temperature of a fever when stuck up a sphincter.

The instruments enable everything readable to be read about the digestive disorders of the winds, the colly-wobbles of the clouds and their cousins the raindrops that variously fall to fertilize the earth or plummet and pour down in such numbers that the population explosion they are always going on about on the radio unconsciously comes to mind.

But scientists and meteorologists, yes all the people who receive the data from the instruments and analyse them; surely they too sometimes have rough days filled with doubts?

For despite all the insights they have gained into mathematical formulae, few things still indeed prove as difficult for them as following in the footsteps of weather-wise farmers, in short of everyone who with invisible eyes sees through the hills and dales of the atmosphere.

For no one has yet managed to harness the vocal chords of birds as meteorological stations broadcasting live the winds, clouds and rain, even though the little white meteorological stations can certainly be seen as a subconscious yearning in that direction.

The Stratosphere's Election Promises

All of which is mentioned here because here beneath the fog-grey clouds that hover ponderously . . .

In rain with drops that never disappear . . .

Here there is little of greater note than the very weather reports that with their optimistic outlooks overshadow almost all other programmes on the radio.

Not just news from distant continents.

And not just sports stories, songs and dance music.

But Bible readings and bird of the day as well.

So it should not come as any surprise that, among the politically informed, weather reports are often called the stratosphere's election promises, nor that in some homes and sundry barbershops it is sometimes joked that they are the work of a vindictive weather god.

Be that as it may and no matter what scientists and meteorologists say and whatever nonsense you hear on the radio, one thing is certain, that as long as they fall either in drizzle or clear and silver, the raindrops don't care two hoots for all the forecasts about the innards of the atmosphere, for they have fallen continuously and unrelenting for so many days and nights that no one recalls any more when they first picked up their drumsticks and began their globular percussion.

Yes, each rainy day has been such an exact replica of the others that in retrospect they all appear to have been a single selfsame day.

Closed for the Summer Holidays

So the afternoon now approaching brings general surprise, but because it was Anton the barber who first saw the blood that flowed in its wake it is only fair to begin the account with him standing, freshly awoken with the glow of morning in his eyes, and because he is holding a cardboard sign in his hands it is also right to mention that the cardboard sign is oblong and white.

He walks across the carpet carrying the cardboard sign, stops by the door and hangs it on a nail by the windowframe so that the bold letters printed on one side of it face outwards.

And what is it that the cardboard sign says, short and sweet:

CLOSED FOR THE SUMMER HOLIDAYS

For the edification of all passers-by.

Also of the raindrops and the grey, hovering clouds.

Yet it is debatable whether so many children have ever been at the barbershop as precisely later that day.

Then it is quite a different kettle of fish that it does not matter which season is in the air outside Anton the barber's windows, and he does not even need to be going to tidy up as he intends now, for if he suffers a stomach upset or slips out for lunch, lies down or has to see the shoemaker on some business or other, the barbershop is always closed for this same reason: the summer holidays.

Yet everyone in the quarter knows that Anton the barber has never gone on what anyone else would call a holiday and in his head the words summer holiday must mean everything else he does apart from cutting hair.

And that day which it was much later attempted to explain on the basis of various peculiar, unpredictable events and to that end even with reference to holy books and ancient sagas . . .

Yes, let us get that quite clear.

Since nine o'clock, Anton, when you customarily pull back the latch to unlock the door; since then the cardboard sign has been hanging in the shop-door window and the barbershop has been closed.

Birthday Parties by the Dark of Night

And that morning.

As the law decrees, the raindrops fall and, in rainclothes with rubber lapels, in wellington boots and with variously yellow or green sou'westers on their heads, the pre-school children have begun to stream past the barbershop and up the steep slope.

First they walk right up the entire slope. Then, on reaching the top, they turn left and walk straight ahead in the direction of the children's chapel where they know that the Reverend Daniel is waiting for them by the swing doors at the front of the church.

The first thing the Reverend Daniel makes them do as soon as they appear is to remove their sou'westers. Despite the fact that the apostles were fishermen, the Reverend Daniel seems to have acquired an allergy towards sou'westers, for sometimes he tears them off the children so frenziedly that they stand completely dumbstruck and fail to take his message on board. Sometimes, moreover, he even wants to undo the bows himself; it is as if he does not feel at ease until all the sou'westers are hanging gaping and empty on the pegs.

Once the Reverend Daniel gripped the strings on one of the pre-school children's sou'westers too roughly, and the boy lost control of himself, ran amok, ran out of the church in his stockinged feet and told his mother when he got home that the Reverend Daniel had been trying to steal his sou'wester.

But if the sou'wester business had been the only thing the children found unusual about Daniel these days there would scarcely be reason for making light of it, because the pre-school children often also wonder if the years in his life are like God's: a thousand years as one day or that kind of thing.

Some of them think, moreover, that it is his birthday every day and he gives parties by the dark of night, for suddenly Daniel has begun to grow so much older and turn so grey that his swollen cheeks, which were always so rosy and happy, have now gone pale and sunken.

And his eyes.

Or more precisely, the bags under his eyes.

At first the pre-school children thought Daniel had walked into the doorpost or the swing doors to the chapel had somehow swung into his face and given him two black eyes.

Except that the rings beneath his eyes . . .

Instead of turning yellow and fading away, they suddenly began to grow and waxed round at first like the man in the moon, until they protruded and since that day have been like bags or potatoes cut in half.

The Arrival of the Ducklings

How is that?

Didn't all this old age begin the day the Reverend Daniel came and handed back their ducklings?

At least, that day will never leave the pre-school children's minds.

Naturally above all because of the ducklings.

But not just.

No, also because that day the pre-school children first noticed that his dark-grey locks with their handsome quiffs were suddenly much lighter than they had recalled them being.

Daniel's hair.

What a sight.

It was not just ruffled but almost as white as the white-haired usher's at the cinema where they were always showing the film about the elephant family.

Besides which he was limping, and that morning the Reverend

Daniel turned up late, which had never happened in all the combined history of pre-school teaching.

Then the children started putting two and two together and even thought that with his limp and white hair, the man who turned up late there was not even Daniel at all.

No way. They got the notion that, like in *The Three Goats* or *Little Red Riding Hood*, a ferocious wolf had broken in to the vicarage and eaten both Sigrid and Daniel and then disguised itself as Daniel to be able to eat them as well.

But no sooner had the children begun to entertain these thoughts than they heard his voice and fortunately he was suffering neither from a cold nor from a sore throat, for the moment they heard it they knew this was Daniel.

His purring, clerical tones were their good old selves and his words, like warbling hymns on the tip of his tongue, they too dispatched their intended role, for the children were as sure as sure can be that no wolf could ever manage to imitate the Reverend Daniel's voice, not even if it took elocution lessons or called in at the baker's.

So it was the colour of his hair, above all else, that lingered like a curious question in their heads, and no one should think that bad intentions guided the boy who got up from the hard pew and asked Daniel, with a serious expression on his lips and his eyes full of deep reflection, how much it costs to have your hair bleached.

When the Reverend Daniel heard this question it transpired, of course, that he had not looked in the mirror before going out, for he looked inquisitively at the boy and clearly felt he was inquiring on his own behalf, for he replied, after looking him over for a good while, that it was quite unnecessary for such a young lad, with such a lovely head of hair, to be worried about its colour.

And on speaking these words Daniel got down to work, limped among the wooden tables and handed back the ducklings which the children had awaited with such expectation and excitement, and they were instantly so enchanted and delighted by the ornately lettered passages from the Scriptures and the hymns and comments that the colour of Daniel's hair had faded completely in the shadow of the ducklings and the mountains and the suns and so they even forgot to ask him why he was limping like that and walking as if his path were strewn with sewing needles.

The Peacocks of Solitude

Indolence in the Working Day

Maybe the clouds scatter sleeping pills all over the quarter.

At least, Anton the barber feels the lamp-posts are yawning on the slope outside the windows, and when the cars outside the houses drive away they leave only their emptiness in the air.

So it is not easy to get down to business, but since Anton the barber has decided that his shop is closed today for the summer holidays and because he has made a decision regarding cleaning, he opens the broom cupboard where the plastic bucket, rubber gloves and mop are at hand.

Notwithstanding, or perhaps precisely because of all the equipment he sees, Anton thinks to himself that the best thing is to start by heating up yesterday's soup and having some coffee and smoking a Salem, for the jobs do not go away even if they are left for a while and by definition anyone who has closed for the summer holidays must have plenty of time.

Yes, Anton thinks something along those lines and when he is sitting in the barber's chair shortly afterwards in the middle of his coffee, cigarette and faded yellow cinema programme about an unemployed circus clown who prevents a girl from committing suicide, and as he watches the fish in the tanks beside the glass shelves performing their tricks and hears the raindrops falling outside the window with a lethargic beat like melancholic jazz, at the same time as, with one eye, he sees the clouds hovering like a framed picture in the windows; yes, Anton the barber feels so comfortable sitting facing the mirror and smoking, drinking, reading, watching and seeing, that he half forgets himself in the interplay of his daydreams and is almost asleep again when there is a sudden knock on a door inside his brain and he leaps to his feet.

In dazed confusion Anton looks at the clock and thinks as he sees the hands that the time has come to put a stop to this lounging around.

Yes, why close for the summer holidays if you don't get down to business, for enough time is spent doing nothing during the working day as it is, without letting it get hold of you in your spare time as well.

Oliver Twist

But, Anton, you must have nodded off, for when you decide to get down to work and begin to put on the rubber gloves and wield the mop, the pre-school children have long since hung up their rain-clothes and the first group that flowed in a straight line past the swing doors has gone and the next is sitting with bowed heads and hands clasped while the Reverend Daniel's morning prayer plays around the cool air of the children's chapel.

Or right up until the point when he says 'amen' and the heads rise and fingers open up again. Then he introduces the hymn which is always sung after the prayer, before the story, for as long as the oldest children can remember; yes, right from the time that the pre-school lessons began and developed into an educational form in their own right, the Reverend Daniel has read *Oliver Twist* aloud to all the classes and groups, and he knows it so accurately off by heart that it does not matter if he occasionally forgets to take along his old torn and tattered copy with Sellotape on its spine, since by the reckoning of wise men he has read this treasure of English literature no fewer than six hundred times, and it goes without saying that he always pauses in the same places, not only to smile, whimper or cry, but to take advantage of the exciting plot and always stop right in the middle, the moment when the children's ears are at their most curious, and then, when the need for words is greatest and the awareness of the magic of letters sharper than ever – at that moment, he begins teaching them to read.

The practical benefit of this technique can perhaps best be seen in the fact that most of the pre-school children are very capable readers when they start attending the white school and it is sometimes even claimed that it is there, on the white wooden chairs of the primary school, that they enter their first relapse.

Hymn Music in the Making

When the reading class is over only the lesson for the day remains, which always begins with a short passage from the Scriptures. Daniel always selects the subject and passage to fit the children's mood and he is in the middle of a lesson about Noah and the Ark and the Flood with the penultimate class of the morning when his wife Sigrid wakes up in the double bed in the vicarage.

On these grounds alone, as Sigrid grasps with one hand at the emptiness where Daniel is not to be found, it is patent that his absence, the Reverend Daniel's disappearance from his double bed, is not the result of his having been swallowed by a vacuum or vanishing into thin air or absconding, but rather because Sigrid, yet another morning, has overslept.

Either Daniel has forgotten to wake her when leaving the vicarage or she has gone back to sleep after he left, because the previous evening she was determined to wake up at the same time as him to make a fair copy of his draft hymn music.

For a short while her eyes close again and for an instant Sigrid feels herself drifting into sleep anew, but her body gives a jerk and her heart jumps to make her start up wide awake at the same time as the swing doors are flung open in the children's chapel.

A few minutes later she is sitting in her nightdress at the kitchen table and while she waits for the kettle to boil she looks out of the window at the ponderous grey clouds and the raindrops and thinks how similar they all are to each other, the mornings in this quarter of town.

The Illusion of Mirrors

Anton the barber noticed as soon as he started scrubbing the walls, which instead of being ivory white were a yellowish brown, and the lino, which instead of being yellowish brown was black, that in fact he had allowed the mirrors to delude him into magnifying the task before him and had been dithering and lounging around as a result.

For it is a fact that the configuration of large rectangular mirrors gives the barbershop an effect of being as much as twice its actual size and the most perspicacious of people have even been known to believe that there are two adjoining barbershops in the basement of the house on the corner of the slope, run by identical twins.

Be that as it may, as soon as Anton the barber begins to dip the scrubbing brush into the boiling soapy water and starts to see the fingerprints of lost moments and the footprints of days gone by disappear, he feels a unique sensation branching through his veins, a sort of cleanliness of the soul, as if not only the yellowish-brown gunge was running from the walls but also that his mind was being made pure.

One after the other the plastic buckets disappear out through the basement door where the light-brown water flows like a muddy river down the iron grid in the drain and the walls are suddenly clean enough to pass for marble statues at an art gallery.

But Anton does not simply make do with washing the walls.

After he has removed the pea-green canvas with its beach sand from beneath the tailor's dummy with her sunhat, the lino will reclaim its original colour and become yellowish-brown again.

And let there be light and there was light, for effortlessly all the muck disappears beneath the stiff hairs of the brush and, Anton, the next thing you know you are standing in a pristine hall and when you fetch the mat to dip it into the boiling soapy water you are close to somersaulting for joy.

The mat seems to travel backwards through time and become new anew as its moments dissolve, so that you, Anton, cannot avoid thinking that the whole history of the barbershop is flowing away, and feel that, before progressing any further, the time has come to go through into the back room, stretch out and take a rest.

Herbert the Headmaster's Propensity for Feeling the Cold

In the beginning was the Word. And the Word was with God . . .

It is not only the case, to recap, that most of the pre-school children who have spent the winter sitting on hard wooden benches at the long tables in the chapel are completely literate when they begin their education at the white school under the direction of Herbert the headmaster, for they are also so well versed in the Bible that their knowledge might more accurately be described as theological training, in many cases so comprehensive and detailed that in the school assembly hall where Herbert the headmaster's rostrum stands in its accustomed place beside the handrail on the stage, and the national flag hangs red, white and blue, and the piano the music teacher sometimes plays is also situated . . .

Yes, it has befallen there on more than one occasion and more than two occasions that little brats have risen to their feet and snufflingly given the vicars who are sent to teach religious knowledge such a grilling that they have been driven off to where Frimann the caretaker, like a malevolent imp or grinning devil, has slammed the door behind them.

So there is nothing extraordinary about the cited words of the Gospel or any other of its passages being heard or quoted in the corridors of the white school, and for those of an understanding and tolerant disposition who bear in mind all other circumstances prevailing there it is not strange either that in the course of time the above-mentioned passage has been distorted so that instead of saying, 'In the beginning was the Word. And the Word was with God', it is said instead, 'In the beginning was the Word. And the Word was with Herbert', and instead of the continuation 'And the Word was God', comes simply: 'And Herbert never shuts up.'

If the truth be told, Herbert the headmaster who sits in his study in the school with a taxidermized gyrfalcon behind him to one side and an illuminable globe on the other is no run-of-the-mill blabbermouth, and were he not the headmaster of the white school but a member of parliament instead there is not an iota of doubt that the record five-hour speech made when Iceland joined NATO would be condemned to obscurity and not be a record any more at all.

Herbert not only gives speeches to the pupils and teachers in the white school; he is also a member of three discussion groups, two debating societies and a regular guest speaker at meetings of all political parties, where it is said he is always put down as first to speak and even phones the chairman of the meeting the evening before to get his name down, for when Herbert has a rostrum in front of him that really means that no one else will take it unless Herbert is cut off in mid-flight.

This, however, never happens in the white school, for no one else is ever down to speak there and the notion of shortening a speech is about as familiar as a still-undiscovered species of fish in the sea.

So everyone knows that any day when Frimann the caretaker's cowbell heralds the approach of a speech, the class that follows will be left as paralysed as a society rent by a prolonged national strike.

In other words:

In a hall with no open windows absolute silence reigns. In mid-speech, perfectly innocent houseflies have been known to become crazed with claustrophobia and commit suicide, and teachers to perspire so heavily from tobacco starvation and lack of stamina that the acrid smell of sweat never leaves their shirts afterwards, and it is common knowledge that almost every time Herbert gives a speech one of the pupils faints, while a number have collapsed in spasms and one bitten out his own tongue.

All the result of the stuffiness caused by Herbert's propensity for feeling the cold; for if all the windows are not closed and carefully fastened by their latches, you can bet your bottom dollar Herbert will begin to sneeze and shiver as a rash of red spots like measles strews itself across his face.

But there are explanations for everything and Herbert the headmaster's propensity for feeling the cold is no exception from that rule, for had he not taken part in a rhetoric contest held by a youth organization the year the Republic was established, there is no telling whether this propensity for feeling the cold would ever have crossed his path like a black cat or speech-making would ever have become his subject, for the story goes that Herbert had been speaking in the contest for more than five hours without a break, outdoors in the pouring rain, and that only he and the panel of judges wearing woollen sweaters and rainclothes had remained when he was seized by such a sneeze that the words ceased to stream out of his mouth and instead flowed out through his nose, through his nostrils, with such force that not only were all the panel's papers blown away to kingdom come, but for all they could see Herbert had sprouted a moustache.

The Banks of Cloud Arrive

The Mysterious Disappearance of a Rostrum

So you could really say that a sneeze sneezed at a youth organization meeting long ago, a sneeze as old as the Republic of Iceland itself, still moves over the face of the waters.

Which is why Herbert the headmaster's speechifying is described in detail here, at the very moment that Anton the barber is resting and Sigrid is arranging herself at the round table in the vicarage parlour to make a fair copy of the hymn music . . .

Yes, what is that echoing with its ding-dong along the school corridors, what but Frimann the caretaker's cowbell calling the pupils into the assembly hall?

And is it not obvious, since this is around noon, that by far the greatest majority of pupils are on the school premises?

Both those who attend in the mornings and according to the timetable may therefore leave, and those who are in the afternoon and according to the timetable are arriving, and just as the aforementioned are trying to rush away the lattermentioned intend by the same token to turn back.

Hustle and bustle.

Back and forth along the corridors, like a flock of sheep in a film, the pupils spill.

But because Frimann the caretaker has locked all the doors and is trying to stand guard at most of them in his own person, no one manages to leave.

For there is no escape.

No, the pupils cannot just jump into Anton the barber's dream nor make themselves invisible and sit like elves around Sigrid's parlour table, or, in other words: face to face with Herbert the headmaster's plans, imagination is almost powerless.

And the assembly hall is soon full and judging from Herbert's grin he looks fairly pleased with the attendance.

And the silence.

It makes a solemn appearance the moment he waves the index finger of his right hand.

Herbert begins by welcoming the fact that the rostrum has been found at last and to tell the truth the pupils were also surprised to see it after such a long absence, because for many weeks the rostrum had been lost beyond recall and Herbert has been forced to speak without his rostrum beside the handrail, and no one has been able to give any information of its whereabouts and the only known fact has been that it disappeared the same night that Siggi's shop was broken into.

In other respects the school authorities have not managed to establish the time of the rostrum's disappearance, to say nothing of succeeding in catching those who removed it, and all the time they have turned a deaf ear and refused to believe the accounts of pupils who claim that on the night in question they heard the cowbell ringing.

And what is more:

Of the sixteen pupils who have been especially under suspicion and been continually interrogated for three whole break times a day, no fewer than seven have admitted to the mysterious disappearance of the rostrum and set off accompanied by teachers from Herbert's study, but without being able to point out the hiding place or return the rostrum in any fashion.

Furthermore, the park has been combed and the beach, the fields and the ditches around them, they have been searched all over, in the stairways of the apartment blocks and the laundry rooms of houses and it was in fact only by pure coincidence that the rostrum was found at all.

One afternoon when one of the geography teachers happened to be passing the broom cupboard in the basement he saw one of the cleaning ladies standing there bending over, enabling him to look up her skirt.

Which is precisely what he did.

He stood there for a long while peering up the cleaning lady's skirt and if she had not moved aside it is by no means certain that the geography teacher would ever have noticed the rostrum, all covered with cloths.

But the cleaning ladies had not returned the rostrum because from the day when its disappearance was discovered they were on strike and for the two weeks' duration of their strike the broom cupboard was never opened and the matter was never resolved either when the strike was settled, for when they saw the rostrum in the broom cupboard the cleaning ladies simply thought that Herbert had got himself a new rostrum and they were supposed to use the old one as a cloth rack.

So they hung a load of dishcloths along its edges and left the floor cloths to dry on the wooden surface against which Herbert sometimes presses his fingers and rests his palms.

The Epidemic of Peeping Toms

On the rostrum there are also rings left by coffee cups and a number of burn marks from cigarettes and as Herbert the headmaster talks a rancid smell of floorcloths sometimes seems to engulf his senses, because every so often a moody scowl crosses his face.

None the less, the stream of words flowing from his lips and around the stuffy assembly hall is such that when Anton the barber wakes up in the room at the back of his barbershop after sleeping for two hours Herbert is still standing at the rostrum and speaking.

And at the same time as the pupils in the hall feel dizziness flickering between their eyes like the flames of candles, Anton thinks, as he gets up and stretches, that now it is about time to get down to work.

First he polishes the mirrors and washes the barber's chairs, the chairs to wait in and the table in front of them, then rubs the glass behind which his diploma is framed and changes the water in the aquarium and dusts the Brylcreem jars, tubes of hair gel and shampoo bottles.

Then it is the turn of the cute-faced mannequin heads that sometimes hang on sticks in the windows, and Anton begins by taking off their wigs and putting them in a soap solution in a little plastic bowl, then mixes hot and cold water in the sink and puts the cute-faced heads to float in it.

Time passes in this way and when Anton has finished polishing the pegs on the coat rack, cleaning the electric shavers and washing the red rubber teats with the barber's scent and arranging the combs in their box, all that remains is the perpetual darling of the quarter, the bald tailor's dummy, who needs to be tended and groomed.

So Anton takes the sunhat off her head, removes her brassière and bikini bottom and takes down the floodlight that customarily dangles above her head and illuminates the sand on the sheet of canvas, so that some customers of the barbershop have the impression of sitting on a Mediterranean beach.

Anton will never forget the day he went to the auction and bought the tailor's dummy.

This was shortly after the draper's shop went out of business and it is true to say that because of the close links the tailor's dummy had with the quarter it would have been a sin against heritage had it been sold beyond its boundaries.

Disregarding various minor events such as the time a gang of teenagers kidnapped her in order to conduct biological investigations in a baiting shed down on the beach, it is the epidemic of peeping toms that broke out among the bachelors in the quarter that is undoubtedly the most famous of the numerous incidents directly attributable to the tailor's dummy.

The epidemic started shortly after the car crash, once the draper's shop windows had been whitewashed over; while the draper's shop was still in its prime, bachelors had often congregated in the parking lot in front of the shops in the evening, preferably beneath a full moon, just to admire her and make acts of worship to her figure, and it is a well-known and well-documented fact that some of them had written poems to her and sent them in to the lonely hearts' column.

That was the way it had been ever since the bachelors began renting lonely garrets in the quarter and right up until the day the tailor's dummy disappeared behind the whitewash, shortly after which the bachelors reappeared at other windows where other female figures, not so tolerant and liberal with their beauty, had enthralled their minds.

It was precisely at this time that the naked postman wearing only a necktie appeared, and both the nude botanist and homosexual milkman were uncovered, but no matter where, all over the gardens of the estate, bachelors could be seen running with their pants around their ankles, and whenever the women from the basement flats looked outside to admire the stars, the Milky Way and Northern Lights, they thought they could see flashers in overcoats and dangling members thirsty with desire.

Only the children seemed to appreciate these antics, calling the bachelors 'Santa's little helpers' and even asking the Reverend Daniel why they were all running around naked at that time of year.

Amusing as this could be, it was not only that many women were getting highly strung; husbands too began to feel their interests were threatened, and some of them took appropriate action, pouring out of the houses armed with clubs and wielding blunt instruments.

Such a decision is not remarkable in itself, and most of these incidents would simply have been forgotten had these husbands and family fathers not made such a bad job of driving the bachelors out of their gardens.

For the simple reason that it fell to the lot of the temperamental telephone engineer, who also suffered from mental disturbances, to nab the first bachelor, whom he did not make do with beating with a club but also cracked his head so hard against the wall as to smash his skull.

When this happened, Anton the barber felt the turmoil and hatred had gone far enough, and the moment he heard about the auction of the complete contents of the draper's shop he resolved to get his hands on the bald tailor's dummy and set her up in the corner by the wall where his diploma hung, to the left of the outermost barber's chair, so that anyone who wanted to contemplate her had to visit the barbershop and have his hair cut as well.

The Banks of Cloud Arrive

By purchasing the tailor's dummy, Anton the barber not only ensured peace in the gardens, but also won himself countless new customers . . . and now as he holds her naked in his arms wondering how best to attend to her personal hygiene and where to keep her until everything is back in its old place, he has a clever idea.

So he lifts her on to his shoulder, carries her across the yellow-brown lino, opens the door and places her beside the corner drain beside the steps down to the basement, so that beneath the raindrops the tailor's dummy looks as if she is standing naked taking a shower.

At this juncture Herbert the headmaster has stopped talking at the rostrum in the white school and it is around the time of day when the coffee breaks in creosoted sheds are either finishing or starting, so that bureaucrats all over the city must be beginning to take sideways glances at their watches.

Likewise this is precisely the moment Sigrid is finishing her fair copy of the hymns, and when she stands up from the parlour table she feels afternoon approaching from all directions and thinks it is best to get the shopping done.

First she dashes something down on to a piece of paper, then puts on her poplin mackintosh and fetches her shopping bag and leaves the house, down the steps, along the paved pathway, past the church bells and down the slope.

Out of the sky, the raindrops fall on the shoulders of her poplin mackintosh and while she is passing between the puddles she approaches the asphalted parking lot in front of the shops, having bought her bread in the bakery and fish in the fish shop, when she opens the large glass door and enters the dairy, where she sees herself in the mirror covering the whole length of the wall and recalls at once that she has encountered this instant before, in a dream.

Inside the children's chapel the Reverend Daniel has often been in the same position he is standing now, alone after the pre-school children have gone out through the swing doors, while they are standing on the gravel in front of the church bells about to set off home when they suddenly stop in their tracks and, as if paralysed with their sou'westers on their heads, peer up into the air as the foggy grey clouds suddenly begin to dissolve and disappear.

Like sheets pulled back, obsolescent stage curtains, or a veil torn from the face of a false prophetess, the clouds disappear and the children think perhaps heaven will open its endless blue doors and the sweet-sounding weather forecasts are about to come true, sending sunny golden opportunities sailing down on silver platters.

In pure rapture, their hearts brimming with hope, they prepare to witness the longed-for sunbeams plunging like champion divers over the houses, to watch them reflect like a volcanic eruption in the windows, thinking that now they must be on the point of coming, because the clouds have gone and the blue sky is there.

But then . . .

Blacker than the blackest of night, the banks of cloud plunge over the city.

Dazed, confused, the pre-school children are struck with bewilderment, and the first notion that occurs to them is that the black banks of cloud are only a cloud of smoke approaching from a heap of burning tyres somewhere in the distance, and they take turns at guessing where the blaze might be, and some of them are even thinking about wrapping their waterproofs tighter and going off to watch the fire.

But then they notice that while they have been wondering, the banks of cloud have not only spread the length and the breadth of the sky, but have also descended to hover just above the roofs, and the children see them assuming the forms of various mythical winged creatures, enshrouding the yellow and green light of the lamp-posts with a fog so black that soon there are neither houses nor apartment blocks to be seen anywhere, and the church seems to disappear.

With their satchels on their backs, sou'westers on their heads, and wearing waterproofs, the pre-school children gear up to make a run for it and rush home like a shot of a shovel, and have just started when the electricity goes off, leaving them unable to see beyond the ends of their noses.

The Dunces' Uprising

Like clockwork.

In an instant . . .

Like chalk from the blackboard . . .

Like the morning dew . . .

Yes, the moment the lights go out and the electricity goes off; in a split second the afternoon yawn disappears from the white school's face.

And the dizziness and dullness in the wake of the speeches evaporates.

And the unease moves from classroom to classroom and spreads with such commotion throughout the whole building that not only do the windowpanes in Frimann the caretaker's greenhouse start to tremble and shake.

No, at exactly the same time the taxidermized gyrfalcon drops off the shelf behind Herbert.

And Frimann's hands are trembling so much he needs only to hold the handle of the cowbell and it starts ringing by itself.

An organized uprising; none of the teachers is in the slightest doubt.

They are absolutely convinced this is the work of the pupils who have asked permission to go to the toilet and used the opportunity to cut off the electricity.

So it is no surprise that canes are gripped firmly and beaten so vehemently on the teachers' desks that when silence is finally restored to the classrooms and quiet descends upon the darkness, no fewer than twelve of them lie broken in two.

Yet the silence is not absolute and the quiet, perhaps it is only the surface impression of what is smouldering beneath; for although nothing is heard from one of the classrooms, more precisely the classroom where the twelve dunces in one of the lowest streams are locked away, the silence is compounded by the fact that the dunces have collectively tied seven scarves around the geography teacher – the same one who a few days earlier found the rostrum and is, if truth be told, neither a scholar nor a gentleman – and bound him up.

This is why the dunces keep quiet, hissing at the geography teacher to be quiet and at each other as well, while each time he looks likely to call for help they brandish torches or tomato ketchup bottles full of sour milk at him.

And they wait with him in the doorway until the moment they can toss him out into the darkness, after which their path lies down numerous steps, down a long corridor past the staffroom and down numerous steps once again, where the broom cupboard appears after one of the dunces has turned on a torch.

After a considerable search they find the key, open the door and politely ask the geography teacher to enter the cupboard, which they promptly close and lock, whereupon the dunces are seen evacuating the white school at a pelt full enough to do credit to whole herd of stampeding horses.

Wide-Open Eyes

Flight in the Darkness

Would Sigrid not just have laughed it off if she had been told that in the afternoon she would meet a green-clad being: a human spectre with icicles that never disappear from his moustache?

But having swept a few round coins down from the smooth white-painted metal counter and put them into a black purse with a golden clasp, and having snapped the clasp shut and dropped the purse out of her palm into the pocket of her poplin mackintosh; yes, Sigrid dallies a good while inside the dairy, standing on its dappled floor waiting for the electricity to come back on and the darkness to flee.

But when neither happens she opens the door and steps over the threshold.

Now the raindrops are falling all the faster and beneath her feet Sigrid can sense the wetness of the asphalted parking lot.

But she sees nothing, and ahead of her everything seems as if she is walking with her open eyes shut.

Yet she still knows when she passes the whitewashed windows where the draper's shop once was and as always when she does so Sigrid remembers the woman who ran the store with her husband before she was killed in the bloom of youth in a car crash claimed by some to be the work of the green-clad being.

But although Sigrid can see nothing and the world in her head is turning like a blind man walking around in circles, she still knows exactly where she is walking and heading.

She knows because she is familiar with the path, every hole, every stone, everything that touches her heels, and she inches her way forward and is a good halfway up the slope when she suddenly hears footsteps that at first come rushing after her, then walk beside her, and heavy breathing.

And because she cannot see anyone she stops, turns around and asks:

Who is that who walks beside me?

Sigrid listens, but hears nothing.

Who is it?

No answer.

The footsteps seem to have fallen silent the moment she stopped.

Or am I hearing things?

Or is the echo of my own footsteps like someone else's?

Sigrid feels half embarrassed about having called out into the darkness to someone who is not there; a shudder runs through her and in her mind the slope turns into a whole age.

Yet she has gone on only a few steps more when she hears the footsteps again, and the breathing, when it draws closer, becomes louder and clearer.

A cold chill plays across her neck and spreads with a terrified expression down her whole body and when Sigrid turns around and sees the glittering icicles and the poisonous glare, she freezes.

Her teeth chatter and she goes all weak and numb, never having entertained the notion she would ever stand facing that man who long, long before the estate was built, had perished in the snow.

He is not only waving a fat horse's shank above her head, grinning, but, as far as Sigrid can see there, is also carrying something under his arm that looks like a woman's head.

She thinks she is falling into a faint, that the blood will soon gush out of her ears, when suddenly the darkness seems to swallow her and to glide with her high into the air.

At least, the next thing she knows she is standing on the gravel outside the benighted church, then hurrying as fast as her legs can carry her across the clover field.

Candlelight in the Shoebox

Yes, such is the darkness engulfing the estate that even though no one has yet reported a seal's head peeking up out of a stove or a pig's tail wiggling in a puddle of mud, it is none the less out of the question to conclude that it is only the pre-school children who lose their way in the darkness outdoors, for the simple reason that people indoors also roam around as lost as if playing blind man's buff.

Anton the barber feels the walls moving by turns into his path or evaporating at his fingertips and disappearing as if the darkness swallows them, and time and again he knocks over the plastic bucket and trips over the chairs before he finally finds the door to his room.

So he kneels down at the threshold and crawls across the floor in the direction of the bed, for Anton knows that if he wants to find the candles he has kept for years in a shoebox beneath the bed, ever since he bought them from a young candleseller who was establishing a candlemaking business in a garage; no, is there any choice but to crawl under the bed and look for the shoebox?

So it stands to reason that after Anton the barber has crawled across the pea-green canvas with sand on it he grabs the outermost leg of the bed with one hand and disappears thereupon under the bed and spends a good while there, for before he manages to get hold of the dusty shoebox in one corner a whole museum of forgotten objects emerges from beneath it.

But so much dust whirls up from the shoebox that for a moment Anton the barber feels as if he has been tarred and feathered, and is surprised how for all these years the shoebox has managed to keep its shape instead of merging into the dust as well.

But if Anton is surprised at the state of the shoebox and the dust on it, his wonder is all the greater when he takes the lid off, not because all the candles have disappeared, melted or assumed curious shapes; rather, all the wicks are burning and the walls in the room light up at that moment like a city bathed in a yellow glow.

Dialling and Dialogues

Who knows . . .

Perhaps we have engaged in conflicts with previously unknown constellations, planets that lonely astronomers have still not located through their telescopes.

Who knows . . .

Perhaps.

Or is it fate that has declared war on us?

Fate driven by the mysteries of primeval forces.

Fate cobbled together from coincidences of varying degrees of ferocity.

Or God, Lord God, have the angels revolted against Thy kingdom and the prince of darkness, is it he who . . .

The Reverend Daniel has been thinking something along these lines as he stands by the windowsill of the vicarage parlour watching the darkness.

Is he thinking?

Or is he not thinking?

That is the question, for every time he thinks he is reaching a conclusion about the essence of the matter the phone rings and parents of the pre-school children want to know what has happened to them.

But the Reverend Daniel has no more idea than they have.

Because he . . .

He who also that day had the children come unto him; he also let them out through the swing doors at the appointed hour.

All that the Reverend Daniel can do is to pray for their well-being . . .

That in their waterproofs they may find their way through the alleyways of darkness and at last discover the path into the heart of the light.

But just as his thoughts disturb his prayers so his prayers disturb his thoughts, and sitting on the dark-brown sofa resting her neck on the cushion cover with Jesus Christ embroidered on it Sigrid disturbs them both, his thoughts and his prayers.

She flickers somewhere between the worlds and in the darkness in the parlour the Reverend Daniel cannot understand in the least why her teeth are chattering like that and why she is ice-cold to the touch.

At her feet lies her shopping bag and she has not taken off her poplin mackintosh, is still sitting there wearing it as she mutters with smothered sobs some incomprehensible words, apparently to a woman Daniel buried quite some time ago.

But despite his intermittent attempts to listen, it is impossible for Daniel to make out what they are talking about.

Raindrops as Red as Blood

All over the barbershop Anton the barber lets the wax drip and fixes the candles so that yellow flames rise up from the glass shelf alongside the mirrors and table, stretching and flickering to make the barbershop, from a distance, look like an elfin city full of lights.

And while Anton sits watching the illuminated aquarium and the fish swimming, he is so enchanted and preoccupied by their colourful beauty that he has almost forgotten the darkness outside when he suddenly remembers the tailor's dummy which surely must have stood long enough in the shower by now.

So he nips out through the door and is about to pull her back in when he is surprised and shocked to find that, instead of standing in the corner by the steps where he had placed her, the tailor's dummy is lying on her side, and her head has struck the edge of one of the steps.

There is a diagonal crack across her temple and a piece has been chipped out of the nape of her neck to leave a large hole in her head, and when Anton bends down to pick her up, for all he can tell there is blood seeping from the dummy's wounds, she is covered in blood.

Terrified, Anton jumps back indoors, for he can well be sure the tailor's dummy has hardly become human just by standing in the raindrops, but at the same time is aware that the black banks of cloud are shedding not only clear silver raindrops, transparent and clear, but also others red as blood and even more green as poison.

So he hurriedly takes the dummy in his arms and closes the door which has only just closed when there is a knock on it and a series of light taps.

Wide-Open Eyes

Time also passes in the darkness.

The shopping bag has been put in the kitchen and the Reverend Daniel has long since helped Sigrid out of her poplin mackintosh.

For time also passes in the darkness.

Now he is standing by the dark-brown sofa, trying his best to calm her down . . . and her teeth have just stopped chattering and Sigrid has started to talk and tell her story.

When the telephone rings.

Holding a candle in front of him, Daniel goes over to the telephone table and as he picks up the receiver he hears a voice say the pre-school children have been found.

They had knocked on the door of the barbershop and when their whereabouts were discovered they were sitting there on the floor by candlelight, playing alternate games of ludo and snakes and ladders.

Such is the relief this news brings that when the Reverend Daniel turns around holding the candle, all desperation, his thoughts and his prayers too, everything is over the hills and far away.

Most of all he wants to snatch Sigrid up and dance with her across the floor of the parlour, as they did at the theologians' ball long ago.

But now the memory of the waltzes seems to call forth hymns in his blood and Daniel has a better idea.

Yes, now is the time to drive away all imaginings.

So Daniel gets out the big white best candles, arranges them on the organ, then walks over to the sofa, takes Sigrid's hand and leads her straight over to the organ.

And guess what:

By candlelight in the unelectrified darkness the parish clergyman's creative talents immediately put in an appearance; effortlessly a brand-new hymn flows out of Daniel's gullet.

And at the keyboard, the first thing Sigrid knows is that her feet have suddenly started moving up and down while her fingers search for notes to lead Daniel towards a melody appropriate to his words and style.

There are heavenly legions and angels armed with the word of God, opening clouds and plummeting tears; rhymes and rhythm and alliteration.

Everything is so natural that even when Sigrid feels her thoughts start to soar she can still hear the sound of the organ and her fingers continue to play while she glides over it across the parlour ceiling.

From a distance she sees the candles, the yellow flames spreading out like a sea of fire from an ancient dream and Daniel, she sees Daniel, his musical lips fluttering, and herself, she sees herself on a stool at the pedal organ.

The only trouble is that when she tries to plunge back down, everything turns black and she does not even hear when the organ falls silent so suddenly that the Reverend Daniel is left standing there a goodly while, singing unaccompanied, before he notices Sigrid is lying across the muted keyboard.

Momentarily he has the notion that Sigrid has gone into a religious trance or fallen asleep and started dreaming, and he is about to give her a little prod to remind her about the hymn-writing when he senses her arms are dangling lifelessly at her sides and sees the eyes behind the hair he strokes away from her face: they are open.

Wide open.

Like doors to another world.

Epilogue of the Raindrops

The Hills' Swansong

Chronicle from the Darkness

To describe the fear of the dark that sailed in the wake of the black banks of cloud, it does not suffice just to unearth one of the radio horror plays and wave it around in front of sleepless eyes.

No.

Such was the scope of the hauntings and such was the darkness constantly covering the sky that to locate this fear of the darkness we are forced to go mentally even further back in time.

So far to a time when neither radio sets nor electric light have yet appeared and lonely country boys have figments of the imagination that neither dramatists nor other authors have been able to outdo since.

Fishermen catch three-eyed cod in their nets and the shadows of weary-eyed, wingless birds move across dreamless sleeps, and since the electricity is continually coming back on and going off, people roam the streets as if in the wilderness.

Like lost country postmen in search of cairns to mark their way . . . and because there is no way of seeing street names, lamp-posts, house numbers or car registration plates, people sometimes find themselves forced to knock on unfamiliar doors.

All the same, no one inside even thinks of opening them, for what are these knockings on doors but yet further evidence of the hauntings that are sweeping the city?

Some believe the whole host of ghosts of times past have been reincarnated and see them as clear as day walking around with ancient outlaws' fear of the dark in their eyes.

Others, on the other hand, maintain they have always been present but are simply taking advantage of the power cut and the darkness of the black banks of cloud.

So every knock on a door is so fearsome, all rustling so terrifying, and it is said that in the houses and apartment blocks, even the women of light and easy virtue are keeping their doors closed and, mindful of the ice-cold persecutions of the fishermen, they refuse to lift the latch or even let in hot-footed lovers with bouquets of flowers.

And the uniformed park-keeper; in the evenings he sits alone, hunched up in the dark, and since the leaves always appear to him as green oilskins he no longer dares to walk down the red paths with his torch and keys.

For this reason all the park gates are left wide open and anyone who so desires can go into hiding there, thieves and housewives and consenting adult males, and the worms in the flowerbeds no longer know the park-keeper by sight.

And while the church stares, sorrowful of countenance, out in to the air, and the white school cavorts in fiery emptiness and while batteries disappear from torches and refrigerators are emptied of their own accord, sometimes all the clocks stop at the same instant.

All sense of time is swept away and no one can remember how long the black banks of cloud have been hovering about the sky when suddenly, one morning, they are gone.

The Almanac of the Raindrops

That morning, the foggy-grey clouds are no longer hovering mistily through the sky above the houses; the greyness has turned all colours of the rainbow and the raindrops showering down on the city are neither clear and silver nor drizzly, their beat far from showing affinities to slow, lethargic jazz music.

When daylight rises up out of the darkness like a figure clad in blue it is obvious to everybody that the clouds swimming and lashing with their tails through the sky most resemble gigantic whales.

Spouting and blowing they cavort in the air and fight each other while the raindrops fall so rapidly they sometimes merge into a single blur.

And the wind . . .

It has turned up too, it has paid a visit too, arrived with no sign of wanting to go away again.

Yes, somewhere in the distance of the darkness it has finally managed to find notes for its flute.

Notes audible to all while the drops whirl and the wind blows.

Along the streets, the yellow puddles ripple, whirling up in gushes and exploding with splashes on car windscreens or swirling about and soaring like surf in the air as huge rivers and cascading torrents pour down the slopes.

And the city . . .

The leaking hut.

The naked tree.

The city . . .

It lies drenched, bathing itself like a helpless drunk wallowing in the mud.

Meanwhile the quarter where the apartment blocks rise and four-storey houses stand is like a vast swamp, a pit floating in mud, for it is not only the old hills by the large apartment blocks that eddy and float like quicksand; the large green fields below the four-storey houses are also rapidly turning to marshland.

Word has it that few people dared venture there after the rainy night when the valley was flooded.

The Flood in the Valley

Is this not the same night that the wind rips the roof off the infants' building of the white school and the jetty below the mental hospital disappears out to sea along with most of the fishermen's boats?

Yes, and the night the wind rages so violently between the houses in the alleyways that it not only tears up fence-posts and lofty trees but also tosses garages out into the blue and sweeps away the toothcombed television aerials.

The saddlemaker's workshop trembles and shakes, instilling its neighbours with a vague fear that the whale skeleton will come flying past and the taxidermized fox heads start to bounce about.

But it is all to no avail.

All the gusts, all the wind . . .

The corrugated-iron-clad workshop withstands it all while the saddlemaker sits in his storyteller's chair, singing and drinking and telling the fishermen stories.

However, everything suggests that the drains in the ditches around the green fields are blocked up, for the moment the water reaches the long-haired blades of grass it begins to flood over the sides.

It floods to left and right, to east and west, first over the fields where it fills up the hollows like ponds, then in the other direction on to the bumpy road that lies like an upturned arch, right through the valley.

From there it flows in mighty currents; over the road at the zenith of the arch, under the barbed-wire fence between the trees and through the gates along the red path, and because the wind is so high and the raindrops so ferocious all the flowerbeds with their worms are instantly submerged and the roots of the trees come loose and their trunks are snapped.

Like thin mud the soil spreads over the lawns and pours around the light-grey benches as it overturns the wastepaper bins and splashes against the statues; and the more numerous that the raindrops become, the harder that the wind blows, the more powerful the flood grows as it breaks next through the little windows and floods in to the basement where the potatoes and hoes and watering-cans are kept; everything crashes and thrashes about.

En route to flow on out through the gates and under the barbed-wire fences at the other end of the park, it also destroys the heated greenhouse with its ornamental plants and flows on to the potato beds that take over where the red paths stop and the park peters out.

One by one the potato beds dissolve and the flood runs in such torrents and with such force that nothing could stop it rushing onwards like a mad cat, tearing up three creosoted sheds and two toolsheds before it pours at a terrifying pace out of the park, submerging everything in its path.

The animals on Gunnar's farm gasp for breath; hens, horses, cows and sheep drown, and for a long time it would appear that no living creature has survived and no one is left alive until suddenly . . .

Yes, in some wondrous way . . .

On the corrugated-iron roof of the barn that floats like a raft stands farmer Gunnar and his black dog, bobbing up out of the flood.

The Hills' Swansong

The same can not be said, however, of the lorry driver's lost toe.

That has never bobbed up out of the mud on the hills.

And the wits of the foreman who now writhes about in a strait-jacket inside the mental hospital.

Can anyone claim he will ever reclaim them?

Or all the tools the navvies lost?

It would be interesting to know if anyone has the nerve to dive into the quicksand and look for them.

But since there were once upon a time a lorry driver who lost a toe and a foreman who lost his wits, there were also once upon a time some hills, which, for as long as the quarter could remember, and in fact much longer still, had been in their place, customarily know as 'the old hills'.

It was there that the children from the quarter had busied themselves making pigeon coops and there were two caves where tramps had lived and a bunker made by nature's own hand but concreted inside, and a well so deep that the youngest children believed if you went down it from the hills you would come out on the other side of the planet.

And that is not all, for there were also rocks in the hills, large mysterious rocks where not only the children knew that, although their names were not to be found in the telephone directory or tax register, people lived inside, little people who had existed since time immemorial.

Periodic shouts of laughter could be heard from the rocks, and carousing and song, and it was even thought that an invisible railway network ran between them, and on many occasions children had been invited by elves and dwarfs to enter the rocks where they claim to have seen colourful costumes, gold-embroidered waistcoats, tasselled caps, and national dress.

Sometimes the dwarfs came out of the rocks and helped the children build their pigeon coops, and they made go-carts and assembled tricycles, and everyone knew as well that Anton the barber, although he never mentioned it himself, toured the rocks just before Christmas cutting their inhabitants' hair, and there was more than one person and more than two who claimed to have witnessed an elfin dance on the floor of the vicarage parlour while the Reverend Daniel was holding his Christmas service.

But because the hills were beside the big apartment blocks and because the inhabitants of the big apartment blocks were always complaining how badly they needed a car park, it was eventually decided to level out the hills and prepare a modern car park, asphalted with white lines painted on it.

This decision was not only accompanied by diggers, bulldozers and lorries . . .

No, it also brought along the foreman who would lose his wits, and the teams of navvies he supervised, and as decreed and corroborated by their timesheets they immediately set to work tearing down the children's wooden pigeon coops with crowbars and claw hammers.

But although the timberwork toppled to the ground and they worked against the clock to tear everything down, it was hard to see who were faster: the navvies who pulled the coops down or the dwarfs from the rocks who put them straight back up again.

And no matter how they tried to fill the well, it always remained the same depth, and by the time the bunker finally gave way one of the bulldozers had needed four replacement engines.

But it was not until the time came to remove all the large, mysterious rocks that the human injuries started.

Because the large, mysterious rocks . . .

Believe it or not, they were either as light as snowballs or suddenly turned so heavy that no chains or tackle could hold them.

Like the rock that fell on the driver's foot and took off his toe; yes, it was on its way up on to the back of the lorry when suddenly nothing could hold it.

And a search was mounted at once, the rock was rolled away and the area was combed. But no matter wherever they looked, the toe seemed to have been swallowed by the rock and was never found.

And then it was the turn of the foreman who lost his temper and, while the navvies nursed the lorry driver, ordered the rock to be blasted to pieces and had holes drilled for tubes of dynamite and insisted on blowing it to smithereens personally.

But no sooner had he pressed the plunger down than his overalls and underpants disappeared from his body, and standing there in front of his mates stark naked and foaming at the mouth, he suddenly seemed to snap, started to bark, and ran away howling.

At this point the navvies thought the safest bet was to get out of the way and because they have not turned up for work in the hills since then, the car parks have still not been realized and the old hills are like a pitted pool of mud floating like quicksand beneath the raindrops, where earthquake tremors can be expected at any moment.

Bells in the Wind

The Classical Detour

The drops fly.

The wind blows.

The Bishop is even claimed to have cried on the radio, shedding tears with such mighty sobs that they are still flowing to this day.

Along the streets, yellow puddles ripple, cascading torrents pour down the slopes and all over the city clergymen with sleepless eyes peer into the hearts of their own souls.

While the drops fly.

While the wind blows.

It is common knowledge that the largest lake in the quarter is below the barbershop at the bottom of the slope, where Anton the barber often stands on a chair and looks out of the window at the children flocking to it with their homemade wooden boats.

But now because it is night Anton the barber is not standing at the window and there are no boats and no children at play, only night with flying drops and blowing wind.

And because it is night and because Anton is lying asleep on the red-covered spring bed in his room, he does not know that on account of the flow of mud down the right gutter of the slope this very night, the flood has made a classical detour and instead of running straight down the slope is heading through the hole in the low concrete wall.

From there it flows in mighty currents to the window on the eastern side of the barbershop and it does not take long for it to break in with a crashing sound and flood and pour unhindered down the bone-white basement wall.

But this night . . .

Yes, either Anton the barber is dreaming far less vividly than the occasion warrants, or is sleeping so peacefully that nothing can disturb him, because despite the breaking sounds when the window caves in and the ever-growing pounding of the waves on the floor, nothing suggests that Anton the barber is about to stir.

A long time passes and inside the barbershop the chairs have started swimming and all the magazines are afloat, and combs, tubes and wigs are flying around with towels and cloths, and as the aquariums topple one after the other the cute-faced mannequin heads are left defenceless, and float about like women deprived of their trunks.

And the barber's coat, the old faithful barber's coat . . .

It lies soaking wet somewhere while the barber sleeps.

Sleeps behind closed doors in his room in a dream so deep that even the rumpus and raging flood cannot wake him up until the alarm clock beside the little porcelain statuette of Jesus Christ suddenly falls over and topples from the shelf above the head of the bed for no apparent reason.

Except that as soon as the clock lands with a thud on Anton's head he starts up as if from a nightmare and, Anton, while you watch the blood pouring on to the pillowcase you hear the waves breaking against the door to your closed room.

The Lord's Message

And the drops go on flying.

The wind goes on blowing.

Whatever it wants to fly, it topples over.

What it wants to rise, it raises up.

Only that which is born of nothing can destroy everything.

It makes the grass speak and the leaves whirl, and sometimes when the transmission lines whirr they sound like screeching fireworks.

And it whistles and pipes, swings lines of latitude above its head like the strings of a bass guitar, and blows from all directions at once.

Then the windowpanes rattle in houses, the lamp-posts shake along the sides of the streets and the church bells, sometimes they ring incessantly.

Since Sigrid died the Reverend Daniel, who otherwise is one of the most productive hymn-writers in the country, has not written a single hymn and, for fear that the children might be swept up into the air and rise to heaven in the physical sense, all pre-school teaching has also been cancelled.

So the swing doors neither open nor swing and the church is shut tight while Daniel, beneath the eternal blows of the raindrops on the windowpanes and with the pealing of the church bells continually in his ears, walks in his full clerical regalia around the vicarage.

So alone and deserted that he wanders, stooping, along the hall from room to room with his sorrows in bags beneath his eyes, or kneels at the little altar in the parlour with his palms seemingly glued together and his lips moving constantly in prayer.

He is praying, and so powerful are Daniel's prayers that sometimes the sound of organ music plays around the room and Sigrid appears before him with a host of angels whom he can just discern beneath his eyelids beyond the raindrops on the windowpane.

And when he stands up, his hair a riot and his eyes staring, he hears the bells ringing incessantly in the wind and the drops beating upon the windowpanes and a voice; through the church bells the wind the drops and the windowpanes, he hears a voice that returns time and again each day.

Every time it does, Daniel pricks up his ears, spreads his arms and waves his fingers like crucifixes, for he knows that like the little flower in the hymn and the lost lamb in the folktale he must also surely find the path and find his way out of the darkened alleyways.

So it does not surprise him that on this very day the Lord Almighty should chose to appear with His voice and attempt to reach him with His message.

For here I am your shepherd and servant, ready to walk any winding path . . .

But no matter how the Reverend Daniel pricks up his ears and waves his fingers and clenches his fists, and no matter what he says, shout and call as he might, he is still unable to make out a word and cannot distinguish the meaning of the message nor grasp the Lord's gist.

As if the wind blows the words away and wafts them about like raindrops, mixing them up and distorting them.

But to ensure that the Lord God Almighty does not give up but continues to talk and deliver His message through the windowpanes, and to make certain that He recognizes his shepherd and does not confuse him with other shepherds and other servants, the Reverend Daniel does not just make do with praying and wearing his cassock around the vicarage during the day, but also sleeps with a golden crucifix in the breast pocket of his pyjamas and the Holy Scripture by the head of his bed and, in order not to leave an iota of doubt, a white dog-collar around his neck.

Is he asleep?

Or is he not asleep?

That is the question, for what is a dream and what is the waking state when nightmares full of whirling drops and blowing winds burst with such horrifying terror through the darkness of night, that the Reverend Daniel wakes up so soaked in sweat that he needs to dry the Holy Scripture on the radiator and wring out his pyjamas and his dog-collar, and all this at the same time as he can hear that outdoors, outside the window, is the reality of the dream, the nightmare like a photocopy of itself.

And thus the days pass, thus the nights pass, and it is no surprise if the Reverend Daniel sometimes thinks in the twilight of morning, while he sits at the kitchen table drinking weak coffee and trying to recover his senses after incomprehensible weird visions that have visited him in his nightmares; no, there is nothing strange about him thinking the world is not just engaged in conflicts with previously unknown constellations and that this is not just the work of fate driven by the mysteries of primeval forces and rebellious angels under the leadership of the prince of darkness, but rather that the moment has arrived, the day has come and the flood has started.